PROMISE

Coeur du Bayou Trilogy

Book One

LISA COOTS

This is a work of fiction. Names, characters, businesses, places, events and incidents are either the products of the author's imagination or used in a fictitious manner.

Any resemblance to actual persons, living or dead, or actual events is purely coincidental.

solunapublishing.com

P.O. Box 775
Jennings, LA 70546

ISBN: 099076690X
ISBN-13: 978-0-9907669-0-2

Cover Art: Phycel Designs, INC.
phycel.com

DEDICATION

To my Sun and Stars,
My reasons for living.
And to my Sisters,
By blood and in Spirit,
Don't Stop Thinking About Tomorrow.

CONTENTS

I AM FROM

I am from flat plains of rich fertile soil where rice, beans, and sugar cane grow.

I am from cypress knee laden swamps alive with mysterious sounds.

I am from blue roof tops, plywood covered windows, generators and emergency food when hurricane winds blow.

I am from crisp fall evenings warmed with chicken and sausage gumbo and spring time boiling pots of crawfish, seasoned just right.

I am from wearing shorts in December, trying to remember what snow feels like and summer heat so sticky and humid it's difficult to breathe at night.

I am from candlelit masses to honor the dead, processions of children bearing flowers for Mary and early morning rosaries prayed in French.

I am from Mass on Sunday and unquestionable Faith handed down from my parents.

I am from simply celebrating life when there is nothing else to celebrate, and the happy sounds of fiddles and accordions.

I am from large family gatherings, in joy and in grief.

I am from remembering our heritage and passing it down to our children.

I AM CAJUN.

~Lisa C. Coots

CHAPTER 1

 The bright, clear morning held promise.
Promise, hope, magic.
Didn't every new day?

That's what Claire Hebert was thinking as she looked out the window at the bright morning sun peeking through the trees. Yes, the promise of something new and different.

The start of a new school year was always exciting for her as a child. At thirty-five, it was no different. She had been teaching for over a decade, and she still loved the feeling of the first day of school. The sound of children echoing through the hallways, and the smells of crayons, paste, and wooden pencils made her feel at home no matter her age.

This day held more than just the excitement of the start of a new year, but also the magic of a fresh start. She had moved from the hustle and bustle of the big city to the quaint Louisiana town of Cypress Point, where she had found a small cottage in a quiet neighborhood. Cypress Point was just big enough to hold one Kindergarten through Twelfth grade school, a post office, a grocery store, a few small diners, and several gas stations. The vast plains of farmland surrounding the town reminded her of her own small home town. The nearby river, numerous bayous and swampland brought outdoorsmen from near and far. With the exception of outdoor pastimes, any kind of entertainment was at least a 30-minute drive to a nearby town. Some people might call it boring. A few years ago, Claire probably would have thought it boring, but not anymore.

The city had held promise for her once when she was young and just starting out. She had imagined that moving away from a small town to the excitement of a glimmering city would magically change her life. She had wanted adventure, and got more than she had ever bargained for. So she was back in a small town, ready to start a new job, a new school year, a new life. She smiled to herself as she drank the last of her coffee.

Her mother, Debra, had tried to persuade her to move back home to Mossville, the small town where she grew up, but she couldn't bring herself to make that move. Claire shook her head as she rinsed her cup in the sink. She couldn't go home. Too many people knew her. Most of the older people would remember her as the wild party girl she had once been. To those people she would never grow up. Besides, she desperately needed a fresh start with no baggage. Her mother had been upset, but happy to know she was much closer. Instead of the five-hour drive, she was under three hours away. So visiting would not be such a hardship on either of them. Not that they visited often. Her mother had finally remarried, a nice man with children of his own. The instant family, including grandchildren, kept her too busy for out of town trips.

A scratching at the door roused her from her thoughts. Rosie, her Great Dane puppy, was ready to be let back in the house. She needed space to stretch her legs. A real plus for her that the cottage she had found had a nice size yard along with a reasonable price. At six months old, her legs were already quite lanky. The cramped apartment they had left behind had Rosie constantly knocking things over as she grew. Judging by the size of her paws, chances were she was not even close to full-grown.

As Claire went through her getting ready for work ritual of dressing while listening to Fleetwood Mac, she mentally prepared herself for the day. The familiar music reminded her of her childhood and calmed her. She hoped that she wouldn't feel awkward. Not around the kids, of course. That had never been a problem with her, but other adults could make her feel a bit self-conscious. Especially since she was the new comer to a small town where everyone knew everyone else, and all of their families, and relatives, blood or by marriage. She mentally scolded herself. Isn't that exactly the kind of place she wanted to be: A quiet place with no surprises? A steady, simple life where she would be at peace? A place where she actually knew her neighbors? Well she would. She knew it wouldn't take long either. In the few weeks since she had moved in, Claire had several conversations across the yard with the Bertrand's, a pleasant, elderly couple that lived next door. She had no doubt they had already filled in the rest of the neighbors on her marital status, background and general health.

Claire laughed out loud as she brushed her dark brown hair until it shone. It was quite comical the way they had shamelessly questioned her about her entire life. Nothing seemed to be off limits. The questions ran the gamut from family, childhood, career choices, finances and finally her love life. The fact that she was in her thirties and never had been married seemed to really pique their interest.

"Of course, it's all so different now. Women don't have to get married and have children. It's not expected of them like it was when we were young," Mrs. Bertrand had exclaimed as her husband had shook his head disapprovingly over his tomato plants. Claire wasn't sure if his disapproval was aimed at her lack of a husband, his wife's comment, or the ripening tomatoes.

Claire had let them think that her career had won out over a husband and family. In fact, her life had not exactly worked out the way she imagined. She had thought by now she would be happily married and have at least two children. In her perfect world, that meant a boy and a girl. She couldn't possibly tell them that her lack of a significant other was solely due to the fact that she had finally gave up on finding Mr. Perfect. For her, Mr. Right was not good enough. He would have to be perfect.

She had found that through the years of dating loser after loser, that the early losers probably weren't losers compared to the last one. Richie Denton. He had earned the title of "The King of Losers" over all loserdom. Thinking back, Dean's long fingernails, even though it really irked her, could have simply been clipped. Tom had no sense of humor. Well, maybe there was no help for that. Chad's pussified-pink Mustang was just a car. Oh, there were other issues with him, besides the car. He was a touchy-feely person and way too clingy for her taste.

Her taste. That's what had gotten her into trouble. She always had a thing for the bad boys. If she had been a teen in the fifties, she would have picked some guy with a leather jacket and a motorcycle over Mr. All-American in a heartbeat. Actually she had dated a few of those in high school against her mother's wishes. Sadly, most of them never lived to see 25. Mothers know things. Her mother had even tried to warn her about Richie.

Shame colored her cheeks as she thought back over the past few years. How could she have been so stupid, blind and gullible? She had never even seen it coming. Were there signs she should have noticed?

Probably, when he started asking for money, dimwit, she thought to herself. That was definitely a red flag. When he had asked her to move in together, she had swooned. Really, stars-in-your-eyes, swooned. She thought he wanted them to be together and eventually get married. They would have the white picket fence kind of forever. *Stupid. Stupid. Stupid.*

When he lost his job, she actually felt sorry for him. Claire had thought that his increased drinking was due to his difficulty finding a new job. Little did she know, his drinking and other recreational habits had lost him the job in the first place and finding a new job was not high on his list of priorities. Why should he when she was paying all of the bills? Over the months his attitude had gotten meaner and so had his friends who didn't seem to have jobs either. Her mother, and the few friends Claire did have, told her to dump him. She couldn't bring herself to leave him when he so clearly needed her. How could they suggest such a thing?

Well, it had taken her two years and a few bruises to realize what a mess her life had become. A mess she had let happen. She couldn't put all the blame on him, or even on the neighbors who didn't want to get involved. She had let it happen.

Claire caught herself singing along with Fleetwood Mac. "Yesterday's gone. Don't you look back." She supposed if she had her own theme song, Don't Stop fit her situation perfectly. Her life had been bad but she had never stopped hoping and dreaming of tomorrow. She had spent the last three years saving to make a break from that "yesterday". She had done it. This was her "tomorrow". Now she was here in a new place where no one knew about her colossal mistake named Richie. She had a fresh start, and if she wanted a white picket fence she could damn well buy her own. In fact, that's the first thing that had caught her eye about her new home. The cute white picket fence enclosing the yard made it easy for her to imagine her and Rosie living there. It made her no never mind if she had nosey neighbors. There was nothing to spy on. She had no love life. Hell, she couldn't remember the last time she had sex, much less a date. Yes-siree, the Bertrand's could pretend a convent had moved in next door.

Claire checked her appearance in the mirror one last time before she picked up her keys and said goodbye to Rosie. Her dark brown hair was just starting to sport a few gray strands. Maybe she should color it? Her blue eyes complemented the turquoise of her three quarter length sleeve blouse, and the modest black knee length skirt hid her not so flat stomach. At 35, nothing seemed to be flat or smooth anymore. Even though she'd never be mistaken for a supermodel, she had accomplished the look she wanted, a prim and proper schoolteacher right down to her Mary Janes. She giggled all the way to her car as she thought that most nuns don't even wear habits anymore, so she could be mistaken for one. Rosie peeked through the front window as Claire backed out of the driveway.

Claire waved and pretended that Rosie was wishing her luck on the first day of her new life.

CHAPTER 2

The first few weeks of school went more smoothly than Claire could have imagined and she quickly fell into a routine. Mornings consisted of coffee, a quick breakfast, letting Rosie out, more coffee, getting dressed and heading out to school. Her class was filled with wonderful young minds, so full of imagination and promise. After school, she went home to Rosie, graded papers and made dinner. It was a simple but welcome existence. When she was out in the yard with Rosie, she would say hello to the Bertrand's if they were outside. She was also making a few friends with some of the faculty at Cypress Point High. Claire smiled to herself as she sat on her porch enjoying what was left of the afternoon. She was happy. Really and truly happy.

She had also been excited to learn that the town held a Halloween festival every year. It sounded as though the whole town participated. If the town celebrated every holiday like that, it would definitely be a big change from the city. She was looking forward to the holidays this year. The other teachers were already planning game booths and other activities. She had been asked to think of a game or activity also. Claire had been thrilled to be included but hadn't thought of anything so far.

Rosie let out a woof, as Mrs. Bertrand wandered over to the fence and called out, "Hello, Claire. How are you today?"

"I'm fine, Mrs. Bertrand. How are you?" Claire answered as she joined her neighbor at the fence.

"I'm ok. This heat is something else though. Just thought I'd check in on you to see how you're doing."

"School is going really well. I have a great class and I'm meeting more people in town. I really feel like this is home." Claire couldn't help but smile when she realized how true those words were.

"How wonderful. We're so happy to have you here. You said you've met some people?" the elderly lady asked curiously.

"Yes, besides the other teachers at school, Tina at the bank and a couple of ladies at the market."

"Oh, I meant men. I was wondering if you had come across my son, Evan. I thought by now you'd have run into him somewhere in town."

Ah, there it was. The reason for the visit. Every time she ran into Mrs. Bertrand during the last week she would mention her son the deputy. She laughed to herself thinking it hadn't taken long for the matchmaker in her to kick in. Claire couldn't help picturing him as an awkward momma's boy. Why else would he still be unattached in a town this small?

"No, I guess not," Claire laughed to herself. "I'm sure I'd remember him but I'm really not looking for a boyfriend. I'm still settling in. Although I did have an offer from one of the male teachers at school. Maybe you know him? Dale Hicks," Claire added hoping to throw her neighbor out of matchmaker mode. It wasn't an exaggeration. He had flirted with her shamelessly every chance he got. She found the attention flattering, but she wasn't ready to date just yet. She wondered if Richie had forever ruined her ability to trust. It's not that she was afraid of men. She just didn't seem to be interested in them romantically. At this point in her life, she was ok with that.

"Oh, he's nice enough. But like you said you're still settling in... You wouldn't want to rush into anything." The matchmaker switch flipped off suddenly. Too suddenly. Claire could tell by her face something was bothering her. She hoped she hadn't said something to offend her new neighbor.

"I'm really excited about belly dancing classes. Have you seen the flyers around town? I'm thinking of joining. It sounds like fun. Tomorrow's the first class," Claire said hoping to lighten the mood.

"Hmm, yes. I guess so. It's supposed to rain tomorrow," she said obviously distracted.

"Are you alright?"

"Yes, well, I guess I'm just worried."

"Is the weather going to be that bad?" Bad weather made Rosie nervous. Claire hated not being there to comfort her when the weather turned stormy.

"Oh, no. Family stuff, dear."

"It's not Mr. Bertrand, is it? Is he sick?" she asked worriedly. The elderly man had quickly become a father figure to Claire. She never knew her own father, so she really didn't know what having a father was like. He had left when she was just a baby. Mr. Bertrand never said much, but seemed like someone you could rely on. He had brought her vegetables from his garden and even cut her grass. A father was someone that took care of his family and it seemed to Claire that her neighbor definitely fell into that category.

"No, no. He's fine. I heard from my daughter, Faith, today. Things aren't going well with her."

"I'm sorry to hear that, Mrs. Bertrand. Is there anything I can do?"

"I told you to call me Margaret, dear, and no, I don't think there's anything anyone can do. Marital troubles. Faith will have to work things out for herself. If there's one thing I've learned, you have to let your kids live their own lives. Just being there for them is really all you can do. It's just so hard to watch them struggle." The worry was evident on the older woman's face. Claire wondered if her mother worried about her and her choices. Guilt flooded through her. She mentally added CALL MOM to her to do list.

"I told her if she decides to leave, she can come back here with the kids."

"Well, she's lucky to have you, Margaret. I would love to meet her one day."

"Yes, and the rest of my kids as well." She visibly brightened. "We'll have to cook something and have everyone over for you to meet them. Our anniversary is coming up. We could do something then. What a lovely idea!" Mrs. Bertrand exclaimed excitedly.

"Oh, don't go through any trouble on my account," Claire called after Mrs. Bertrand but she was already planning the menu as she hurried back towards her home. Claire sighed and went inside to call her mom.

Claire was disappointed when she got her mom's voice mail, but left her a message letting her know that everything was going fine. She imagined them all on some family outing, a dinner out or an unexpected shopping trip. *One day that will be me*, Claire promised herself.

CHAPTER 3

Evan Bertrand shook his head in disgust. All six feet and 185 pounds of him was soaked to the bone. This had been the worst day he'd had in quite some time and a reminder of why he prefers the company of dogs rather than people. Normally his job consisted of writing a few tickets, keeping rowdy kids in line, and occasionally a few adults after too many beers down at the local bar. Being a sheriff's deputy and the closest law enforcement in Cypress Point had its perks. He was born and raised here so he knew just about everyone. In recent years, new families had moved here from the city to raise their kids. Even with the newcomers it was still a small town. Hell, everyone knew everyone's business, and as annoying as that could be, it sometimes was a plus. Crime was just about nonexistent. He often found himself helping out the elderly with odd jobs that wouldn't normally be in his job description. That was fine by him. He was here to protect and serve. Technically his duties covered the whole parish and he was called to other areas when needed, but most of his time was spent in the corner of St. Francis Parish where Cypress Point was located. He loved the small town and the people in it even when they got on his nerves. He couldn't imagine living anywhere else, even if he was the dog man.

Cypress Point was also too small to have its own animal control officer or pound. So it fell to Evan to pick up strays. He was supposed to bring them to the Parish Shelter but couldn't bring himself to condemn helpless animals whose only crime had been that they were owned by selfish people. People who dumped them out in the country as soon as the cuteness wore off. He had often found homes for the strays with the help of some of the local animal lovers, but soon had acquired a few canine companions of his own. He decided to build his own shelter since his land was on the outskirts of town. It was far enough out that the barking of his dogs wouldn't disturb the good citizens of Cypress Point.

Today had started out fine even with the rain. Then a call about a fender bender involving a teenage girl had quickly escalated into a domestic disturbance when the mother got to the scene. When Evan had tried to intervene the mother had turned her fury on him. The things that were coming out of her mouth would have made a sailor blush. Evan tried unsuccessfully to calm the woman down and then just decided to take her abuse. He wouldn't have to deal with her for long, but he felt sorry for the young girl who had to go home with her. Then in the middle of the rainstorm he had come across old Mr. McCormick trying to change a flat. The flat was a lot easier to deal with than the fender bender, but now he was soaked and in a foul mood.

When his cell phone rang, he wanted to throw it out the window, but the call was from his mom. He sighed as he pushed the strands of wet jet black hair off of his forehead. He really didn't want to answer it. The last few weeks all his mother's calls included information about her new neighbor. Evan tried his best to ignore the matchmaking and change the subject but his mother didn't give up easily. Let it ring, he told himself. He'd get some coffee and dry off a bit then maybe call his mom back. The guilt crept in as the phone continued to ring. What if something was wrong, maybe an accident with his dad?

He sighed again and clicked the button to answer.

"Hi Mom. What's up?"

"Hello dear. I was just calling to tell you about our anniversary dinner. We decided to barbecue here at the house. What do you think?"

"That sounds great mom. Everything else ok?" Evan asked knowing something else had to be wrong. His mother didn't call during working hours unless she needed something. Asking advice about the barbecue was just an excuse.

"Well, have you talked to Faith lately?" she asked hesitantly.

"No. Why? What's wrong with her?" The mention of his little sister had him instantly defensive.

"I don't know if I should say anything..."

"Well now you have to, Mom. What's going on?"

"I think her and David are about to split up. I told her just to come on home and bring the kids."

"Damn. That sack of shit better not have hurt her."

17

"Now, Evan. Calm down. I think it's just her heart that's broken. He cheated on her again. I don't think he's even trying to hide it anymore."

"I should drive over there and kick his ass. Do I need to go and get her?"

"No, I don't think so, but maybe you should call her."

"Ok, Mom I will. Tell Dad hey for me and I'll try to stop by later."

"Alright, dear."

Yep, he was right. It was surely shaping up to be one helluva day. He definitely saw a drink in his future.

As the windshield wipers scraped the glass, he thought about his sister, Faith. They had been so close growing up even though she was a few years younger. She looked up to him and had tried to keep up with him. Sports, hunting, fishing. It didn't matter what it was. If he was interested in it, she was right there alongside of him. Then she turned 14 and discovered boys. Sigh. He had always been protective of her and very critical of her choices of the opposite sex. They had their share of fights but always managed to patch things up quickly.

Until she had set her sights on one of his best friends, Jake. That didn't sit well with him, and of course ended in one big pile of shit when he opened his mouth about it. He had lost a good friend and his relationship with his sister was never the same. He still ran into Jake from time to time. It was inevitable since they both lived in Cypress Point. They were civil to one another but the tension had never faded. Faith had dated his ex-friend on and off through high school but the relationship didn't last. Faith had went off to college at LSU and ended up marrying David Williams.

What a pompous ass! Fake as the day was long and twice as slimy. Evan couldn't stand him from the minute he met him but didn't dare say a word to his sister for fear of ruining what relationship they had left. Faith had fallen for the plastic smile, showy facade and a ticket out of Cypress Point. He didn't blame her for wanting to expand her world, but damn it there were other ways instead of chaining herself to a two timing jerk. He had been right about him all along, but wasn't feeling too proud of himself. He hated knowing his sister was unhappy.

The rain was coming down harder now. Evan slowed as he debated calling Faith or just showing up and telling her to pack up the kids.

Suddenly a white flash darted in front of his SUV. He swerved to miss...the horse? calf? Almost landing his vehicle in the ditch, he cursed as he put the SUV in park and went out into the rain again. So much for drying off. Shivering on the road was a spotted Great Dane. It didn't seem to be hurt but eyed him cautiously.

Evan called the dog over. It let out a woof and ran to him almost knocking him down. He opened the door to the cab.

"Come on, get in!" he said patting the seat. The dog happily jumped in and sat on the seat as if it belonged there. Evan chuckled as he climbed back in.

"Well, girl. I'm sure somebody is missing you. You can ride shotgun till we find out who."

Evan didn't recognize the dog. It was either a very well cared for drop off or somebody's pet that had somehow gotten loose in this weather. At the sound of thunder the dog scooted closer to Evan and whimpered.

The storm raged on as he decided to stop by the post office. Helen, the postmaster might have an idea of who it belonged to. If she didn't, he'd stop by the diner. Somebody was bound to know where it came from. He pulled into the parking slot closest to the door put the SUV in park and ran inside the building.

"Evan, you are soaked! What brings you out here in this weather?" Helen clucked from behind the counter.

"I found a dog running loose in the street. I don't want it to get hit. You know anybody who has a black and white Great Dane?"

"Hmm, not that I can think of. Those dogs get really big. I'll come around and see if I recognize him."

"It's a *she* and she doesn't like this weather. She's terrified."

A flash of lightning split the sky and thunder boomed shaking the building. Evan heard a yelp. He looked back through the glass door just in time to see the dog flailing around in a panic. One of its hind legs hit the gear shift and he watched in horror as his truck moved forward toward the building. Everything seemed to move in slow motion. Evan called to Helen to get back as he tried to make it out the door. He felt like his legs were made of molasses. Helen was just making her way around the counter when the wall started to crumble. Evan, after what seemed like an eternity, made it out the door, hit the wet cement and nearly slid under the side of the oncoming vehicle. Scrambling to regain his balance he grabbed a hold of the door handle and managed to pull himself up. Once he opened the door and flung himself into the cab, he had to maneuver around the terrified dog. By the time the vehicle stopped the damage had already been done.

Claire jumped at the sound of the thunder as she left her classroom for the day. It had been storming all day. She couldn't help but worry about Rosie. The big scaredy cat was terrified of bad weather. Claire sighed. She knew she'd have a mess to clean up when she got home. The weather made Rosie so nervous she'd pace frantically around the house knocking things over.

She had stayed after school for the first belly dancing class that was being held in the gym. She was glad not to have to go out into the rain. Hopefully the storm would be over by the time she made it home. Claire had been looking forward to class. Not only would it give her a chance to get to know more people but she would also get to move around. Being dragged around by Rosie wasn't exactly exercise.

As she entered the gym, she said hello to fellow teachers and made her way to the floor. She hadn't been sure what the dress code was for belly dancing so she had brought shorts and a tank top to change into after school. She was glad to see everyone else in shorts too.

"Hi, I'm Serena. Glad you could make it." Claire was greeted by a slender, dark eyed woman with long, black curls wearing a hip scarf over a flowing skirt and bare feet.

"I'm Claire. Very excited to be here." She smiled shyly.

"I don't think I've seen you around town. New

here?"

"Yes, just moved here. I teach third grade. Did you grow up here?"

"Oh, no, I bought an old house out on the river a few years ago. Rumor has it the house is haunted. Everybody still looks at me funny, so I don't come into town often. I guess the belly dancing doesn't help. I wasn't sure what kind of reception I would get." She looked around at the gathering of females and smiled. "Looks like we have a few that were curious enough to check it out. Let's get started."

After making sure the post office was secure enough for the night, Evan had taken the Great Dane home and locked her in a kennel. Then reluctantly headed into the office to file an accident report. He knew the jokes and ribbing would be relentless.

The snickering started as soon as he walked in the office. Thankfully there were only a few people hanging around shooting the breeze with the Sheriff's secretary, Irene. He was sure that he had been the main topic of their conversation. Evan tried to ignore it, but he was waiting for the shoe to fall. Hershey Purcell better known as "Squirts" was on dispatch, his meaty face trying hard to hide his amusement as he swiveled his office chair around to face Evan. The mischievous gleam in his eyes had Evan worried. Hershey was known for being a top notch asshole who relished the pain and suffering of others.

"Hey, Hersh. How's it going?"

"Pretty crazy with all that rain, huh?" Hershey asked trying to sound casual.

"Yeah, it's been a crazy day." Evan tensed waiting for the jab.

"So, where's the new partner?"

"Not funny."

"Oh, but it is and it's going to get funnier. You're about to get your ass chewed. He's waiting for you." Hershey jerked his thumb in the direction of the Sheriff's office then swiveled back to face the game of solitaire on his computer.

"Shit." Evan had hoped to avoid this discussion today.

"Yeah, Evan, keep it up and you'll be the one on dispatch permanently."

"You're just mad cause you're still on his shit list after that last wreck."

"Um, no. You and the driving dog are his shit list today. Lucky for you it's not an election year, you'd be a gone pecan." His wild laughter bounced off of the plexiglass window in front of him.

Evan narrowed his eyes at his back. "You think? I'd have to disagree, Squirts. You've wrecked how many units. Is it 3 or 4? I forget. He kept you around and you're just a pile of shit."

The laughter died suddenly. Evan waited as the big man turned back around slowly. Before he could open his mouth to reply the door to the Sheriff's office opened. Everyone quickly lost interest in the scene and turned their attention back to their work.

"Irene, I said to send him in as soon as he got here," a big voice boomed from behind Evan. Sheriff Kermit Bourque was a bigger than life figure with no volume control. He made it his business to know everyone and spent most of his time politicking his way to sheriff. Now he was cultivating his image. He had recently gone as far as hiring a publicist to help him achieve rock star status. Big fish. Small pond.

23

"Sorry, Sheriff. I didn't want to interrupt," Irene said with a smile as fake as her flaming red hair and nails. "I thought you were still on the phone."

"Evan." The big man didn't wait for a reply. He went back into this office.

Evan followed him in and shut the door behind them.

"What in the hell were you thinking putting that dog in your unit?"

"It was in the middle of the road. I didn't want it to get hit or cause an accident." Evan said lamely as he sat down in a chair.

"And that worked out for you, did it?" Kermit asked as he perched his giant body on the corner of his desk. "You damaged a government building and a cruiser... for a dog, Evan. I know you have a soft spot for animals. That's great and it's given this department a lot of good publicity, but this is gonna hurt. I'm gonna have to do some damage control."

Buzzing from the intercom on his desk saved Evan from the rest of his tirade. Evan knew from experience he was just getting warmed up.

"Sheriff, your wife is on line one." Irene's nasally voice squawked through the speaker.

"Tell her I'll call her back."

"She's pretty upset. Something about the caterer for the fundraiser."

"I'll take it." Kermit sighed as he stood to round his desk reaching for the phone. "Evan, I know it was an accident, but I really need you to keep your head on straight. The last thing I need is another Squirts on my hands."

Evan stood. "Yes, sir." Breathing a sigh of relief as he walked to the door and opened it.

Waiting until Evan was half way through the door Kermit called out in his booming voice, "Oh and Bertrand.... Try to remember, we put the criminals in the *backseat*."

Riotous laughter erupted from the outer office as Evan shut the door giving everyone a dark scowl. Evan knew the jokes were just getting started and he didn't see an end in sight. The up side, his SUV was still drivable. There would be some body work to be done, but right now he just wanted to file his report and go home. A hot shower, hot food, and a cold beer. Maybe not even in that order and make that several beers. Yep, this day was one for the record books and he was ready for it to be over.

CHAPTER 4

Claire was glad the rain had slowed to a drizzle as she parked her car in the driveway. Ouch, she was going to feel those hip lifts for a while. A good soak in a tub of hot water would definitely be needed tonight. *Who would have thought belly dancing would be so strenuous?* she thought as she unlocked her front door. She put her bag down on the couch and looked around. The lamp was knocked over but not broken. There were books scattered on the floor. Well, the mess wasn't too bad. She was lucky her furnishings were sparse second hand flea market finds. Her living room only held a small, well-worn sofa, two mismatched chairs, and a small round side table that she had originally purchased as a nightstand. Through the years, she had moved it where ever she needed it. It had probably been used in every room of the house.

Whenever she felt like a change, she would buy bright colored pillows and a new throw to cover the lumpy sofa. It wasn't very fashionable, but it was her favorite place to snuggle with a good book.

Claire tried to bend down to reach for a book then groaned in pain. The cleanup could wait. She sighed as she looked around. She would love new furniture but it had taken every cent of the money she had secretly squirreled away to make a decent down payment on the house and pay the moving expenses. She didn't mind. Over time she could find things to fill her home and make it look the way she wanted.

She walked to the kitchen dreaming of colors she would like to paint the walls. A crunch under her feet stopped her in her tracks. Dog food was scattered all over the floor and the back door was wide open. Rosie! Claire ran out the back door calling for her. When she didn't find her in the yard, she went back into the house to make sure she wasn't hiding under the bed. One of their favorite games was hide and seek.

"Where's Rosie?" Claire called hoping the thunder had the giant lap dog cowering under the bed.

Rosie was nowhere to be found. Claire's hips hurt and her stomach was in a knot as the tears rolled down her face. Rosie was her baby. What if she got hit on the road? What if someone took her? Claire tried to calm herself. She went back outside and walked up and down the street calling for Rosie. When she didn't come, Claire decided to drive around town looking for her.

She drove slowly street by street looking in yards. It was dinner time so everyone was in their homes winding down after their busy day. As she drove by the school, she saw Serena heading to her car, so she pulled into the parking lot. Serena noticing her, stopped and waited for her to roll down her window.

"Hey, did you forget something?"

"No, I'm looking for my dog. I got home and she's gone. I've looked everywhere and I can't find her." Claire could feel the tears forming again.

"Ok, it's ok. I'll help you find her. What kind of dog? I'm sure someone must have seen her." Serena smiled reassuringly. Claire described Rosie explaining her fear of bad weather.

"Look, leave your car here and I'll drive you in my car. You shouldn't be driving. You're too upset."

"Ok. You sure you don't mind? You don't even know me," Claire said sniffing.

"Not at all. We'll find Rosie. I think if we go by the diner and ask, maybe we'll have some luck."

The brightly lit diner had quite a few people enjoying their food in cozy booths. Looking through the window at the various groups of families and friends all smiling and laughing made Claire feel more miserable. All she had was Rosie. What if she didn't find her?

"You stay here. I'll go ask around," Serena said as she patted her arm.

Dale Hicks was leaving the diner as Serena walked up to the door. He looked her up and down then up again. The sly smile on his face almost made Claire laugh. When Serena smiled back at him and started talking to him, he instantly stood straighter and puffed out his chest. Ugh. She couldn't believe she had actually considered going out with him. No, her judgment in men definitely couldn't be trusted. She watched them talk for a few minutes, then Serena rushed back to the car. Dale's eyes followed her ass all the way. When he looked up at the car and saw Claire sitting there his face turned beet red. He immediately turned away.

"Mr. Cheesey said it sounded like the same dog that got picked up by the 'dog guy' that lives going out of town with the kennels. I know the place. I pass it all the time on my way into town," Serena said as she closed the door and started the car.

"Dog guy?"

"Yeah, some crazy guy that has a lot of dogs."

"Is that all he said? He was practically drooling." Claire snorted.

"What? Oh, yeah, he was trying to be smooth. I escaped before he asked me out. Eww. What a slimeball."

"Yes he is."

Serena turned to her wide eyed. "Oh my god, You know him? I'm sorry."

"Don't be. Story of my life. Apparently I only attract jerks. He teaches at the school. I'm glad I never actually agreed to go out with him."

"Well, it seems as though Rosie is the talk of the town. Something about an accident or a wreck or something."

"Oh No! She's got to be ok." Claire sobbed as she imagined Rosie being hit by a car. "She's all I've got."

"Hey, you've got me now. Besides, I'm sure she's fine. Let's go get her," Serena said reassuringly.

A few minutes later, they drove up to a ranch style house. From the look of things no one was home. The driveway continued past the house to the kennels.

"Let's drive all the way up to the kennels to see if she's there," Claire suggested. As the car lights swept across the fenced area Claire held her breath willing

Rosie to be ok.

"That's quite a few dogs in there. Oh wait. Is that her?" Serena asked.

Claire couldn't spot her among the gang of barking dogs. Then she noticed her over in a kennel by herself. It was Rosie!

"Yes, that's her!" They jumped from the car and hurried to the fence. Rosie jumped up at her name and began barking.

"How do we get in?" Serena wondered out loud.

"Look, the gate's over here."

"Shouldn't we knock on the door or wait for someone to get home?" Serena looked around nervously.

"I want my dog! He had no right to take her and lock her up like this. Look at all these poor dogs. What kind of person keeps so many dogs like this?" She huffed as she pulled on the gate. It was locked. Rosie yelped.

"We've got to get this open. I'm not leaving without her," Claire said desperately as she yanked on the lock.

Serena's face lit up.

"I've got it."

"Got what?" she asked doubtfully. Claire wasn't sure she liked the glint in Serena's eyes, but was glad for the support.

"I've got bolt cutters at home. Let's go get 'em," Serena said excitedly.

Claire was hesitant to leave Rosie. "Ok, you go, but I'll stay here with Rosie. This guy sounds like a creep."

"Ok, stay here and I'll be back. My house is a few miles down the road. But it shouldn't take me long.

There's not much traffic out that way," she said as she hurried off to her car.

"Just hurry. I don't want to be here when 'dog guy' gets home."

Claire watched Serena back out and drive away. Without the car lights she couldn't see much and instantly regretted not going with her new friend. The lone security light by the house shone across the driveway leaving the kennels in shadows. The other dogs calmed down a bit once Serena left but watched Claire cautiously. Rosie's whimpering broke her heart. As far as she could tell, the outer fence gate was locked but the smaller cell Rosie was in was just latched. If she could climb over the outer fence she could at least get to Rosie to comfort her.

CHAPTER 5

Evan was just getting out of a much needed hot shower when the dogs started raising hell. He sighed. They were just probably showing off for the new girl. Since he wasn't sure how the other dogs would react to the new guest Evan had put her in a kennel by herself. Of course, Red and Scruffy were letting him know they wanted to come inside. They had been with him the longest. Both strays that had wandered into his yard, skinny and pitiful looking. Red had actually been hurt but the leg had healed nicely. He barely limped anymore. Evan had made the mistake of letting them in at night when it was just the two of them. They liked curling up next to his bed when he slept. Now there was just too many of them to have in the house. Every now and then he'd still make an exception for the original two.

Tonight he really didn't feel like company, even of the canine persuasion. He dried off and walked to the kitchen to grab another beer. He had downed the first one as soon as he walked in his door after parking the wrecked SUV in the garage. Ok, *hiding* the wrecked SUV in the garage. He didn't need every looky-loo passing by to see what kind of damage the driving dog had done. He groaned again. He knew people joked about his dogs and called him crazy. He didn't care about that, but this was another matter entirely. He took a swig of beer and glanced out the kitchen window in time to see a car backing out of his driveway. *Great!*

That's what had the dogs in an uproar. If it was that nosey lady from the local newspaper, he'd probably lose his mind. She had called him several times today wanting to get a picture of him and the dog in front of the post office. He didn't want to piss her off. She had been real good about posting pictures of the strays and helping to find them homes but he wasn't about to pose for a picture in front of the demolished wall of the post office. His pride could only take so much.

He went to his room and grabbed a pair of jeans tugging them on as he made his way back to the kitchen. When he looked out the window again, the car was gone and the dogs had quietened down. Sighing heavily Evan turned back to reach for his beer hoping there would be no more unexpected visitors. Those hopes were dashed when a fresh chorus of barking sounded. Someone was out there. He grabbed his gun and slipped out the back door quietly.

Claire's second try at climbing the fence was going better than the first. She had tried climbing up the middle but realized too late that the chain link fence couldn't support her. It moved and sagged, first inward then bowed out, beneath her weight making it hard to keep her wet shoes gripped in the holes of the fencing. The racket she made triggered another round of nervous barking from the pack of dogs within the kennel.

"Don't laugh at me," she muttered in frustration, "You can't climb a fence either."

Trying again closer to a post for support Claire was making better progress. She was halfway up the fence when she heard a deep voice say, "Hold it right there."

She lost her footing on the slippery metal and slid down the length of the fence. She landed on her butt with a splat onto the muddy ground. Expecting to see some redneck with a beer gut, Claire looked up and nearly gasped out loud. Standing over her was a gorgeous, shirtless, dark haired man holding a gun. Her brain short circuited. It didn't seem real. *He could be in a movie. He definitely works out.* Thoughts rolled through her head. Hot steamy thoughts. The rain started coming down harder. She blinked the droplets away and her eyes focused on the gun he was holding at his side. Her brain screamed *RUN!* So she did. She scrambled to her feet in the slippery grass and took off. She could feel mud squish under her feet. Her hips were screaming in pain as she ran blindly in the rain.

"Are you fucking kidding me?" Evan growled as the woman ran away. He tucked his gun in his waistband and went after her. She didn't get far. Evan tackled her to the ground. Cursing as he held down the struggling woman.

"Hold on, Damn it. I'm trying not to hurt you."

"Get off of me you maniac!" Claire said trying to

push him off of her.

"Stop!" He roared.

She looked into his fierce dark eyes and froze. Claire hated herself for that submissive reaction. Years of screaming and intimidation had her trained to submit. Richie would scream and smack her around until she backed down. After a while it was automatic. She would just shut down when he raised his voice.

"Who are you and why were you climbing my fence?"

"My name is Claire. You have my dog. I want her back," she said without emotion.

"Ok, Claire," he said over emphasizing her name. "You were planning to climb the fence and then what? Throw the dog over and climb back out?"

"No, I was just going to calm her down," she said in a small voice. It had seemed like a reasonable course of action at the time. Now she felt foolish.

He shook his head in disbelief as he stood and helped her up. She was now soaked and covered in mud. Her tank top was plastered to her body showing off the curve of her breasts. He made an effort to look back up at her face.

"And just how were you planning to get out? Or were you going to wait for me to find you here locked up with the dogs?"

"No, my friend was coming back for me," she mumbled.

"Ah, the car I saw driving away. Why would your friend leave you here?" he said trying to put the pieces together.

Claire looked down at her muddy shoes.

"She went to get bolt cutters for the lock."

He barked out a sarcastic laugh. "Well, you had the jail break all planned out, didn't you?"

"I just want Rosie back," she sniffed.

"You can have her back. I don't want your dog. I'm just curious. Did it ever occur to you that you were trespassing? All you had to do was knock on the door. You could have been shot!" he yelled. Claire couldn't raise her head to look at him.

"Damn, I need another shower," he muttered looking down at his muddy jeans.

"I just want my dog back," Claire whispered.

"I just want this day to end." Exasperated he grabbed her arm and led her back to the kennels.

By the time Serena's car pulled back into the driveway, Claire was trying unsuccessfully to dry off with one of Evan's towels. He had left her at the kennels to get her a towel from his house. To her disappointment he had also put on a shirt. Claire gave up trying to dry herself and wrapped the towel around her shoulders. Evan was liberating Rosie from the kennel, when Serena rushed up with the bolt cutters. She came to a halt when she noticed Evan.

"There's the accomplice," he said dryly as he walked Rosie out of the kennel gate. "You're the one that bought the old Amie place out on the river. Should have guessed y'all weren't from around here."

"Oh, well, I guess we don't need these." Serena blushed and put the bolt cutters behind her back.

Claire, happy to be reunited with her dog, bent to hug Rosie. She ran her hands over her twice before she was satisfied the dog was unharmed.

"No, ma'am. You don't. I guess I should be comforted in the thought you had to go find them. If you had them in your trunk I'd have to wonder if this kind of thing was a habit for you two," he said gruffly.

"Sorry. But no harm done, right? Claire gets her dog back, and everything worked out." Serena flashed a bright smile at him.

"Save it, sister. You two were trespassing on private property. I could file charges."

"What?" Claire's head snapped up. *What an asshole!* "Charges? If anyone should be filing charges it's me. You took my dog, and locked her up. Then you pulled a gun on me!" She took a step toward him.

Serena paled. "A gun?"

"You make it sound like I stole your dog and was holding her for ransom. She was running in the street. That's neglect!" He closed the space in between them. "Never mind the fact that you two came in my yard without my permission and planned to damage my property. Trespassing. Vandalism. I'm well within my rights to protect my property. I could have shot your ass right off of the fence, lady!"

"Whoa! Hold on, you two," Serena said as she stepped in between them.

"She loves her dog and was worried. You obviously love dogs too. So you can understand," she said to Evan. Then to Claire, "Yes, we should have waited for him to get home, and if we would have used the bolt cutter we would have paid for the damages."

Evan took a deep breath. "I said I could file charges. I didn't say I would. The point is y'all can't go messing around on other people's property. It's a good way to get shot. I'll get my truck and drive you and Rosie home."

"We can ride back with Serena. My car's at the

school anyway," Claire argued.

"No use getting her car all muddy or making her drive back into town. Besides, I want to make sure you and your dog don't cause any more trouble tonight."

"What's that supposed to mean?" Claire asked, indignant.

"She got out once today. I want to make sure it doesn't happen again," he said over his shoulder as he headed to the garage.

"Oh, right," Claire said and stuck her tongue out at his retreating back.

"Are you sure, Claire?" Serena asked hugging the bolt cutters to her chest as she enjoyed the view.

"Yeah, just call to check on me later. He's a jerk, but I'm not getting axe murderer from him," she answered sarcastically.

"Mmmm. Yeah, but what a fine jerk he is," Serena said still watching him walk away.

"Oh, please."

"Like you didn't notice he's a hunk," Serena teased.

"Oh, I noticed alright. But, gee, I don't know, the gun in my face kind of killed the mood." She looked down at her wet mud encrusted clothing and sighed. "Something tells me I didn't make that great of an impression on him either."

They looked at each other and started to giggle.

CHAPTER 6

The ride back to her car was awkward. Claire was still stunned to see the Sheriff's vehicle. She decided it was best not to mention the damaged front end. Her escort didn't seem inclined to talk about the details. Claire figured he had to be her neighbor's son. Wow, had she been wrong. Evan Bertrand was a far cry from a momma's boy. He was gorgeous, but a bully. Don't forget he's also a sheriff's deputy. He could have arrested her. What a nightmare that would have been! She could have lost her job. She considered herself lucky and decided to just thank him for the help. Then stay as far away from him as possible.

He argued with her at the school parking lot when she wanted to take Rosie from there and go home. Since she didn't have an explanation of how Rosie had managed to get out in the first place, he won. When she explained that the back door had been open, he had gotten mad and insisted on following her home to check things out.

He went through the house first to make sure no one was inside. When he was certain it was clear he called her and Rosie in.

"Why didn't you call someone?" he demanded as soon as she walked in.

"What are you talking about? My dog was missing. Who do you call for that?" she snapped back at him.

"Someone broke in your house and wrecked the place," he said pointing out the mess, "Is there anything missing? Can you tell?"

Claire looked around and laughed. "No, this mess is from Rosie. Bad weather frightens her. She does this all the time. I just moved in a couple of months ago so I don't have a lot of stuff yet."

"Are you sure? I don't see your TV." He pointed at the shelves filled with DVD's.

"I don't have one," she said simply.

"Then how do you watch those?"

"I haven't gotten around to getting a new one yet. I use my laptop when I want to watch a movie."

"And where is that?" he asked as he looked around again.

"In my car."

Evan sighed then tried a different question, "You said the back door was open?"

"Yes, it was when I got home. That's how she got out, but I know I locked it before I left," she said defensively.

"How do you figure she opened the door? Then the gate?" he asked as he turned to the kitchen.

"I don't know about the door. The gate I didn't bother to latch because she was inside. Do you really think someone broke in?" She pulled the towel around her shoulders tighter.

"Let me take a look at the door."

She followed him to the kitchen to examine the back door. He yanked it open without even turning the knob. The knob was locked but the latch hadn't caught because the door wasn't closed all the way. The humidity had been so high that the old wooden door had probably expanded. He slammed the door shut and tried again. This time it wouldn't open.

"It probably wasn't closed all the way and the wind blew it open," he reasoned.

He looked back at Claire shivering in the middle of the kitchen. Her blue eyes looked up at him expectantly. He hadn't noticed her eyes before. It had been too dark to notice much besides her shape. He had noticed her bare legs and the way her damp shorts had clung to her backside when she was hanging on his fence. He had definitely noticed her wet t-shirt and the harden nipples that had shown through the material. Now she looked vulnerable with her mud encrusted hair and clothes plastered to her body still wrapped in his towel. The cause of all the trouble, Rosie, sat next to her looking innocent. He took in the mess that surrounded them. Chaos. Trouble. This woman and her dog were a menace to society he reminded himself. He needed to get away from her as fast as possible.

"Make sure you close it all the way," he said gruffly. The dog food crunched under his feet as he stomped out of the house.

Evan noticed his dad was making his way across the yard when he got outside.

"Hey, Dad," Evan called.

"Saw your truck over here. Wanted to make sure everything was ok."

"Everything's fine."

"See you met our neighbor. The girl ok?" He motioned to the house.

"Yeah, I brought her dog back. It had gotten out." Evan didn't feel like explaining all the details.

"Heard about that. Your mom's worried. She had been waiting for you to come by."

Of course, it was all over town. He groaned. "Look, Dad. I've had a helluva day. Tell Mom I'm sorry, but I just need to put this day to bed."

His dad chuckled, "See you later, son."

As he drove home Evan couldn't help think about the events of the day. He shook his head. There was no point in trying to figure out where it had gone wrong. What's done is done, no use in worrying over it. That's what his dad always said. The damage to the post office and SUV could be fixed. The joking would hopefully die down eventually. He would get through it.

His mind kept wandering back to Claire. He had a feeling he was about to have some sleepless nights in his future. Evan wasn't exactly sure what it was about her that was bothering him. Ok, so it wasn't everyday some chick tries to climb into your dog kennel. She was obviously crazy and that's what had him disturbed. He had dated plenty over the years, but never felt the need to get serious. He had numbers of girls that he could call if he felt like going out into the city or staying in for a romantic night. It had just been awhile, that's all. Oh, hell, who was he trying to fool. He had a soft spot for strays, and she had looked at him with those helpless eyes. No, she hadn't been helpless trying to get her dog back. If he hadn't been home he had no doubt that the chain would have been cut and the dog gone by the time he got back. He didn't know what to think about Claire. He just knew it wasn't going to be easy to forget about her.

CHAPTER 7

 "Have you seen him again?" Serena asked as she walked with Claire out to the parking lot of the school.

"No. I mean, I saw a sheriff's car around town, and it was parked next door one day, so I'm sure it was him. The SUV must be in the shop."

"I can't believe he hasn't been by or at least called you." Serena looked around as if willing him to appear.

"Why on earth would he call me?"

"Look, I pick up on stuff like this. He was definitely interested."

"I trespassed on his property. My dog wrecked his car. And I can't believe he saw me looking like that. When I looked in the mirror that night, I couldn't blame him for making a beeline for the door. I looked like a drowned rat. No, worse than a drowned rat," Claire said miserably.

Claire had been horrified to learn it had been Rosie that had wrecked into the post office. The lady from the newspaper had wanted a picture of Rosie for the paper. She had also been thoroughly embarrassed to learn about Evan's shelter. The newspaper lady had done nothing but sing his praises. She couldn't say enough about how he helped strays find homes and people donated food and other items to help him out. She still couldn't believe she had practically called him a weirdo dog thief. In her defense, that was before she knew he was a cop.

Margaret had been at her house the very next day wanting to know about their meeting. She didn't have the heart to tell her exactly what had happened so she just gave her vague answers. Claire knew Evan would probably be happy to give her the full scoop about her crazy neighbor.

"Want to get something to eat?" Claire asked her friend brightly.

"Sure, but you're not changing the subject. I'll meet you there." Serena winked at her and headed for her car.

Once they were tucked into their booth at the cafe, Serena started in again.

"I'm telling you. He's got the hots for you, and I *know* you're interested in him."

"How many times do I have to tell you? I'm not ready to date."

"Yeah, yeah sure. That's what you say, but I know better. You just wait and see." She gave Claire a knowing smile.

"Hey, speaking of *'Knowing All'* have you thought about my booth for the Halloween festival?" Claire asked hopefully.

"Yeah, about that, I really don't mind helping and all, but I don't know about the card reading. People already look at me funny. I'm finally getting to know some of the ladies because of belly dancing. I don't think I should."

"Oh, come on. I told some of the other teachers and they loved the idea. Seriously. It'll be fun and I don't have any other ideas. Everything else is taken. I really need you to help me with this."

Over the last month they had become close friends. Claire had missed having someone to share stories and secrets with. After their amazing dog rescue, she felt like she could trust Serena. She had even told her about Richie. No one else in town knew about him and that's the way she wanted it to stay. They saw each other at least once a week at belly dancing class, sometimes more and talked on the phone quite a bit when they weren't working.

"Um, ok. Yeah, that'll be fun..... and we could really dress up the booth, right? Make it look like a real gypsy tent."

Serena's sudden change of heart and nervous chatter had Claire suspicious. She was looking at something over Claire's shoulder and was obviously trying to distract her.

"Yes, that's what I was thinking. I'm glad you decided to do it," Claire said before she could take it back. Then she looked over her shoulder through the window. It was Evan. He was walking down the street with a dark haired woman and two kids; a boy and a girl. The kids ran in front and stopped at an old truck. Claire watched as they all climbed in and drove off. She felt like she had been punched in the stomach. She knew she had no right to feel that way. He probably hadn't given her a second thought or if he did it probably wasn't a happy one. She had heard some of the jokes going around town. Most of them directed at Evan. She knew it was all because of her. Why would he be interested? She had done nothing but cause him grief.

When she looked back at Serena, she could see pity in her eyes.

"Don't say a word," she whispered.

"Oh, Claire. I still say it's going to happen."

"Stop. Ok. Just stop. That's why I haven't heard from him. He's seeing someone. Now you know," she snapped. Claire had been thinking about him more than she cared to admit. She had hoped to run into him somewhere, just to see how he'd react. She hadn't seen much of Margaret lately, but if truth be told she'd been avoiding her neighbors. She was still embarrassed by all the trouble Rosie had caused.

"They weren't holding hands or anything. I'm sure they're just friends," Serena pointed out.

"Look, I don't care." Claire hid her misery with a cheesy smile and waggled her eyebrows at her friend. "Let's talk about our fortune telling booth."

"What?" Serena looked confused, then remembered their conversation. "Oh, right. I don't know about that."

"You can't back out. You said you'd do it." Claire pointed a finger at her.

Serena sighed then laughed. "Ok, you twisted my arm. I tell you what. Let's go shopping this weekend for fabric for the tent and we need costumes. I think our booth should be as realistic as possible."

Claire laughed, "Whoa, hold on there. Let's not go overboard."

"If we find some fancy drapes we like we can use them for the sides of the tent, then I can hang them in my house. I'll buy them."

The excitement in Serena's voice was contagious. That was one thing she admired about her new friend. When she decided to do something, there was no holding back. She jumped in with both feet and enjoyed the experience no matter what the outcome.

"We'll have to make a budget," Claire insisted.

"Well, we can at least look around for ideas. A shopping day would be fun!"

"Yes, it would. Can we make it Saturday? Sunday is the Bertrands' anniversary barbecue," she said, her excitement deflating, "I had already said I'd go. At first I was excited about it, but now...." Claire sighed and dropped her head.

"We'll go Saturday. While we're out, we'll get you an outfit to wear on Sunday."

"Oh, no. I think I feel a cold coming on." Claire faked a few coughs into her hand.

"Oh, no you don't. We're going to find you the perfect outfit to get his attention. I promise."

CHAPTER 8

Claire turned in the mirror. The dress Serena had talked her into buying was beautiful. Not something she would have picked out for herself, she admired the colors that had been hand painted onto the material. The swirls of blues and greens faded into the off white background only to reappear in other places. It was magical the way the fabric clung where it needed and flowed where it shouldn't. The design really flattered her body and the belly dancing had definitely helped get her back into shape she thought as she turned again. The silver strappy sandals glinted in the light as she turned. Serena had justified their purchase by announcing they would be part of her fortune telling costume.

Claire was amazed at how great she looked but was still a nervous wreck. She knew Evan would be there. Would he bring the girlfriend? Claire wished now she had ran into Margaret. She could have found a way to ask about Evan even if Margaret didn't volunteer the information. She thought if Evan did have a girlfriend, Margaret would have definitely wanted to talk about it. Unfortunately, she must have been busy planning the barbecue because she hadn't seen her neighbor in over a week. If the thought of not showing up to the barbecue had crossed her mind, the note stuck to her door reminding her about the party guaranteed she'd have to at least put in an appearance.

Suck it up, girly, she thought to herself as she took one last look in the mirror, patted Rosie on the head and went to the kitchen to pick up the pasta salad she had made to bring with her.

As she crossed the yard she saw a few cars and people already gathering, so she hoped to slip in among a group and not draw attention to herself. Margaret spotted her right off and took the salad from her into the house. Claire thought about following her into the house to hide, but decided it was best to get over seeing Evan straight away. She couldn't help herself, she wanted to see if he had brought a date. She knew she shouldn't care but wanted a closer look at the girlfriend.

Claire said hello to the people she knew and chatted for a few minutes with each. She finally spotted Evan over by the barbecue pit. He was staring at her with those dark eyes, an unreadable expression on his face. She turned to make sure no one was behind her, then turned back. He was still staring. Not sure what to do she smiled at him and waved. He gave her a nod and turned his attention back to the meat.

OOOkkaaay, that was uncomfortable, she thought as she scanned the groups of people looking for anyone she knew. Two kids ran by her chasing each other around the side of the house. The same two kids she had seen with Evan that day in town. Her stomach did a somersault. She looked back at Evan to find he was watching her.

"Hey there neighbor," Mr. Bertrand spoke from behind her.

Happy for a distraction she turned and greeted her neighbor. "Happy Anniversary!" she said as she gave him a quick hug.

"Thanks," he muttered as his wife popped out of the door behind him.

"Claire, can you please bring this over to Evan? He'll need it when the meat's ready," Margaret said handing her a large pot.

"I can bring it," Mr. Bertrand said as he reached for the pot.

"No, I need your help inside, dear." His wife slapped his hand away.

"Sure, it's no problem. Just let me know if you need help with anything else. I don't mind really," Claire said glad of anything to keep her from awkwardly standing by herself.

"You are so sweet. I have everything inside ready, if you can just help Evan." She smiled sweetly. Then pushed her husband back to the house.

"Of course." Claire put on her best smile and walked over to the barbecue pit. Evan watched her approach.

"Hi! Your mom sent me to bring you this and said I'm to help you out," she said trying not to sound too nervous.

"And you fell for it." Evan laughed.

"What do you mean?"

"Don't tell me she hasn't been talking to you about me...," he said with a smirk.

"Why would she do that?"

"Look, I know my mom, and I know she's trying to get us together. That's why she sent you over here." Evan hoped he wasn't being too harsh. He had been dreading this day ever since the last time he saw Claire. He had been successful in avoiding her, but knew there was no way around it today. His mother would make sure of it and she had. What he wasn't counting on was Claire looking so damn good. He had never seen a dress like that but knew not every woman could fill it out the way Claire did. He had a hard time not thinking about her since he met her. Now it would be impossible.

"Oh, yeah, she did at first but not anymore. I figured since you were seeing someone....Never mind." Claire stopped herself from running at the mouth. "Let's start over. So, how are things with you?"

"Got my vehicle fixed. My pride might take a little longer." He grimaced.

"I'm really sorry about all of that. I was hoping I'd run into you."

"Pun intended?" he asked snidely.

"What?" Claire asked innocently then catching his meaning blushed. "Oh, no. I meant I was hoping to see you."

"Really? Why is that?" His dark eyes narrowed as he watched her.

"I wanted to apologize."

"For?"

"Well, it was Rosie that caused the damage and it's my fault she got out." He looked at her expectantly.

"And for trying to break her out." Evan was just staring at her, so she kept talking. "And for not being very nice. I'm afraid you may have gotten the wrong impression of me."

"What impression would that be? Crazy dog thief?" He laughed.

"I'm trying to apologize," Claire said sincerely.

"Apology accepted," he said as he started taking meat off of the pit. "What's done is done."

"You must be the neighbor I have been hearing so much about." Claire turned to see the same woman that had been with Evan in town. She had really only seen her in profile while getting into the truck, but the impression she had gotten was one of beauty. Up close she realized her impression had been right. Her dark almond shaped eyes regarded Claire curiously.

"Um, yeah. I'm sure Evan filled you in on the crazy dog lady that lives next door." She smiled waiting for the jokes to start.

"Well, then you two do make the perfect pair. Everyone calls him the crazy dog guy." She laughed good naturedly slapping Evan on the arm.

"Knock it off, Sis. Claire, this is my little sister, Faith."

Faith? Oh, God, she felt like a complete idiot. She had completely forgotten about the sister but now that they were standing next to each other Claire saw the resemblance. She was so glad she had stopped her blabber mouthing before she had embarrassed herself further.

"I'm surprised Mom hasn't introduced you two yet," he said suspiciously.

"Stop being so paranoid. It's so nice to meet you, Claire. I'm sure I'll be seeing you around since we'll be neighbors, and the kids will start school here tomorrow."

"That's great. I mean, I'm glad you're here. Your mom and dad must be thrilled that you and the kids are here."

"Yeah, they've been really great," she said biting her lip. Her eyes suddenly sad and wistful looked around to find her kids. She shook her head then smiled at Claire again.

"That dress is amazing! Isn't it, Evan? Doesn't she look fabulous?"

"Thanks," Claire muttered suddenly feeling very self-conscious.

Evan nearly choked on his beer. "C-cah-hadn't really noticed." He looked at her now and nodded. "Yeah, it's great."

"Wow, you are such a liar!" Faith laughed. "He hasn't been able to take his eyes off of you since you got here. Dad's afraid he's gonna burn the meat."

"No, I'm not gonna burn the damn meat. In fact, here. You can take this inside for me now," he said holding out the pot to his sister.

"I'll do it," Claire said thoroughly embarrassed. She felt her face redden and couldn't escape fast enough. She grabbed the pot from Evan and hurried off to the house.

"Gee thanks, Sis. Way to make her feel welcome." He frowned at his sister.

"I wasn't the one ogling her. Sorry, I just couldn't help it. I think it's funny."

"What's funny? Embarrassing Claire?" he growled. Faith caught his tone and thought to herself, *He's got it bad, and he doesn't even know it.*

"Ha. It's funny that somebody has finally caught

your attention, and Mom was right." She stuck her tongue at him and ran after Claire.

"Claire, wait let me help you with that." Faith called out. She reached Claire just in time to grab the door and hold it open for her. Claire took a step inside and stopped unsure of where to go.

"Um. Where should I put this?"

"Oh, through here in the kitchen. I thought you knew where it was," Faith said leading the way.

"No, I've never been inside. I usually just visit with your mom and dad outside."

They walked through the laundry room into a roomy kitchen that opened into a dining area then a living room. Claire immediately felt at home. She looked around at the knick knacks and pictures. It wasn't these items that made it a home, Claire realized. She knew it was the years of love and good memories that filled the house. *One day*, she promised herself, *I'll have this, too.*

"Just put it on the counter. I'm sure Mom will be here in a minute to see about it." Faith hesitated for a second then added, "Look, I'm sorry if I embarrassed you out there. I didn't mean to. I was just picking at my brother. Old habit."

"Oh, it's ok. I just don't think he likes me very much," she winced.

"What? I was serious about him staring at you."

"Oh," Claire looked around nervously, "so you grew up here?"

"Yep, born and raised in this house till I moved to college."

"Is that you?" Claire asked pointing to a graduation picture hanging on the wall in the living room.

"Yes, that is me. Don't you just love the big hair? And that, of course, is my pain in the ass brother, Evan."

Claire gazed at the picture. The familiar dark eyes looked back at her. It was definitely him, just a younger version.

"He must have been popular with the girls," Claire said dreamily before she realized she was speaking out loud.

"Oh, yeah, he was. I guess," she answered thoughtfully. Then she pointed to the next picture on the wall, another dark haired girl. "That is the baby sister, Elle. She came along when I was about 9 and ruined everything." Faith laughed. "Do you have siblings?"

"No. I don't. Are you glad to be back home?" Claire asked trying to change the subject. Not being able to help herself, her gaze kept wandering back to Evan's picture.

"I am. I just never thought I'd ever have to come back, but with the kids.... I don't know. It just seemed like the right thing to do, you know. I think it'll be better for them here, with my family around. Well, for me too. I need to figure out where to go from here." She smiled sadly.

"Yeah, I know about starting over. Sometimes it's the best thing," Claire said thinking about her own move. She remembered how terrified she was, but in the end it was definitely worth it. "I'm right next door if you need someone to talk to and I'd love for you to come with me to my belly dancing class. It's so much fun."

"I probably will need to exercise. I've been eating nonstop since I got here. Mom's cooking and all."

She patted her mid-section. "But belly dancing?"

"Tuesday's in the gym. You'll meet my friend, Serena, too."

"Oh great. What trouble are the three of you going to get into this time?" Evan said from behind them. Claire jumped, startled by the sound of his voice. Then turned awkwardly when she realized she was still staring at his picture.

"Trouble?" Faith asked raising an eyebrow.

"Yeah, trouble. I think you'd better steer clear of those two criminals, Sis." He winked at Claire and brushed past, their bodies barely touching but the heat that radiated from them had Claire taking a step back. He disappeared down a hallway.

Claire took a deep breath and put a hand to her heart. It felt like it was going to beat right out of her chest.

Faith laughed wildly. "Ok, you've got to tell me what that was about and it sounds like I'm going to like your friend."

"You mean he didn't tell you? I thought for sure he told your parents." She stared at the empty hallway in disbelief.

"Mom! Mom!" a child's voice yelled from the door.

"That's me." Faith let out a sigh. "I'd better go see what they are up to. But don't you forget you've got to tell me everything."

Claire glanced around realizing she was alone, but Evan was sure to come back out of the hallway at some point. She took one last look at his picture then nearly ran out of the house.

The rest of the afternoon was pleasant. The

October sun was still warm, but the breeze hinted at a crispness that would bring a chill with the setting of the sun. The meal had been delicious, what she had managed to eat of it. Margaret had maneuvered her into sitting next to Evan at the picnic table. Every movement she made had her brushing arms with him. Thankfully Faith and her kids had sat across from them and kept the conversation from being too awkward. Claire got them to talk by asking them about school. Trent was 10 and Hannah was 8. Watching them together made Claire wonder if that's how it had been between Evan and Faith when they were younger. She laughed to herself as she realized they still joked and picked at each other. She did notice that Evan went out of his way not to mention the divorce.

After the meal, Claire and Faith found a shady spot in the yard to watch some of the men play washers.

"Ok, now you can fill me in on why my brother thinks you're a criminal," Faith said with a twinkle in her eye.

"Ugh, it's kind of funny now, but really embarrassing. I'm glad he didn't tell your parents."

"Spill it. I could use a laugh," Faith demanded as she leaned back on her elbows and stretched out her perfectly tanned legs on the freshly cut grass.

Claire fidgeted and smoothed her dress over her not so tanned legs as she recounted her and Serena's daring attempt to free Rosie, Evan catching her climbing the fence and her shameful fall into the mud.

"Then for some reason, I thought I could outrun him. He tackled me, so we were both rolling in the mud." Claire blushed remembering him shirtless.

Faith had tears in her eyes she was laughing so hard. "Wow, I thought the dog wrecking into the post office was funny."

"I just can't help embarrassing myself when he's around..." She glanced over to where he was waiting his turn to throw the washers. He was talking with the other men but his eyes never left hers.

"Mmmm, so did he cuff you?" Faith asked with a wicked grin.

"Oh, no...he didn't." Claire covered her face in her hands hoping no one could hear their conversation. "He was nice enough to take me home, and check the door."

"There's that blush again. Did you want him to cuff you?"

"Stop. You're worse than Serena."

"If that's the case, I'm sure we'll get along great."

Evan didn't know how he had ended up getting wrangled into bringing the dish and food to Claire. Yes, he did. His mom had straight up told him to bring her dish back to her, and a plate of food for supper. She had also loaded him up a plate, too. The other guests had left. Faith was helping clean up and his dad was already in his chair dozing off. So here he was carrying the food to Claire's like his mother wanted. He wouldn't admit it to his mom, but he didn't mind it. He actually had enjoyed being around her today. It was just annoying that his mom was pushing him and Faith kept ragging on him. He just couldn't help being stubborn about it. He did not need his mother setting him up. Did he? Nah. He could find a girlfriend if he wanted. The problem was he had gotten comfortable being on his own. He liked it that way.

He had watched Faith and Claire talking under the tree like they were old friends. Laughing and giggling. It had been nice to hear his sister laugh. He was guessing it had something to do with him, but that was alright. Whatever it was had the color back in her face and the sadness gone from her eyes. When he had driven to Baton Rouge to pick up her and the kids, he was startled at her appearance. The dark circles under her eyes and hollowness to her cheeks had scared him. He was glad David had been out of town. He would have been tempted to beat him to a bloody pulp. With each day that passed she began looking more like her old self. He knew his mother was making sure she ate even when she said she wasn't hungry. They all spent time with the kids when she seemed to need time alone. Today had been better he thought. She had seemed happier. She was really getting a kick out of teasing him about Claire.

Claire. Claire. His mind kept wandering back to Claire. He stood at her door now wondering if she had changed out of that dress, half hoping that she hadn't. He figured what the heck, one more look. What would it hurt?

Claire had called Serena as soon as she got home to fill her in on the girlfriend that turned out to be the sister. The sister that was turning out to be a new friend. She couldn't wait to get the two of them together. Maybe they could rope Faith into helping with the fortune telling booth, too.

A knock on her door surprised her. She was more surprised to find Evan standing on the other side of it. He had barely spoken to her after lunch but watched her with those dark eyes of his. Here he was now carrying her bowl and plates of food wrapped in foil.

"Hi."

"Hey, Mom wanted me to return your bowl and bring you this food. No sense in you cooking with all the leftovers we had."

"Oh, thanks. Come on in."

He followed her into the house admiring the dress once again. She had kicked off her shoes by the door. He noticed her bare feet and painted toes as he followed her to the kitchen. His gaze reached mid-calf before he was nearly knocked to the ground by Rosie.

"Hey girl." He chuckled as he tried to keep her from jumping on him.

"Down Rosie! Here just put that down on the table. I ate so much I probably won't be hungry for a while."

"You and Faith seemed to get along ok. Thanks for making her laugh."

"Laugh?"

"Yeah, it was good to hear her laugh. She's been taking the break up pretty hard. So thanks for taking her mind off of it."

"I really like your sister. Well, your whole family. They've all been so nice to me. I hope that we can be friends too."

"Sure. Why not?" They could be friends. His thoughts had been running to the more than friendly zone. *How often would she wear that dress?*

"It just seems kind of awkward between us. I hope that what happened before won't stop us. I really am sorry for all the trouble."

Girls don't like to wear the same things over and over. She might not ever wear it again. "Stop us?" He absently gazed at the fabric that seemed to be molded to her hips.

"From being friends."

"You already apologized. You don't need to again. In fact, I'm sorry too. I wasn't exactly my charming self. I had had a rotten day and maybe I was a little rude."

"It's ok. So we're good?" she asked as she opened the back door and let Rosie out.

"Yeah, sure." He pulled out a chair and sat at the table. "So what did Faith find so funny?"

Claire immediately started blushing. "I told her about that night. Me climbing the fence, or *trying* to climb the fence and us ending up in the mud."

"Well, I didn't find it funny at the time. I still don't. I could've shot you." He rubbed his hands over his face.

"But you didn't." Claire put her hand on his shoulder. "Come on, I totally made a fool of myself. I don't know what I was thinking trying to climb that fence."

He looked up at her and into those blue eyes. "Damn, we can't be friends."

Next thing she knew she was in his lap, his mouth covering hers. Her arms snaking around his neck. He tensed and deepened the kiss. She melted into him, her mind spinning.

His hands seemed to be everywhere. Claire felt as if she were drowning and needed to come up for air. So she did.

Pressing a finger to his lips, *those lips*, she gazed into his eyes, *those eyes*, and whispered, "I'm so confused. You don't want to be friends?"

"Yes. No. Damn it. I think you need to take off this dress."

"What?" She stood on shaky legs.

"It's driving me crazy. All I can think about is taking it off you."

"Hold on," she said, wishing she had something to hold on to. "My dress?"

He groaned and stood, towering over her. "I'm sorry. Look, I don't know if friends is gonna cut it." He reached out and pulled her close again. This time his kiss was soft and tender, filled with promise.

He let her go and said, "Think about it."

Then he was gone.

CHAPTER 9

Claire spent the rest of the night and most of the next day thinking about it. She kept replaying the kiss in her mind. She'd be thinking of something else only to be reminded of the feel of his lips on hers. In fact she had a hard time concentrating on anything at all. In class, she caught her mind wandering off to Evan. What was he doing? Was he thinking about her? Did he really want to be more than friends? This was crazy. She was crazy. Sigh.

A knock at the classroom door brought her back again. Faith and Hannah walked in smiling.

"I get to be in your class, Miss Claire," Hannah said excitedly.

"Hannah, it's Miss Hebert in class, remember," Faith corrected her daughter.

"I'm so excited to have you here, Hannah. Why don't you get settled and then I'll introduce you the rest of the class," she said as she walked with Faith to the door. Once they were in the hallway, she looked at Faith hoping that she had some information or at least direction.

"What's wrong?" Faith asked looking back at the classroom.

"Umm, nothing. I just thought we could talk in private for a few minutes." Suddenly she wasn't so sure she should bring it up. It was her brother after all.

"Oh, sure. About?"

"Well…," she smiled sheepishly.

"Oh my, is this about Evan going over to your house last night?" Faith giggled and danced around sending her ponytail bobbing back and forth. "*I knew it!* Momma asked him to bring your dish back and he jumped up so fast. So….what happened? Did the lunkhead finally ask you out?"

"Not exactly."

"My brother is so slow," she said shaking her head in disappointment.

"Not…..exactly."

"Then what exactly? What happened?"

"It was crazy. One minute we were talking, the next minute I was in his lap and we were making out like teenagers. Then he said we couldn't be just friends. Does that sound like your brother?"

"Ha! Well, he's smarter than he looks. This is great!" She hugged Claire so forcefully she had to step back not to fall.

"Is it?"

"Of course. So when are you going to see him again?"

"I have no idea. He just said to think about it."

"And???"

"I have thought about little else. I just don't know

if he's waiting for me or if I should wait for him...."
Footsteps echoing down the hallway interrupted their
conversation. They both turned to see Dale Hicks
walking towards them.

"Well, hello, ladies."

"Dale. How are you?"

"I'm fine." He smiled at Claire then nodded in
Faith's direction. "Faith, I heard you were back in
town," he said looking her up and down. "We should
all get together sometime. You know and catch up."

"I see you almost every day, Dale," Claire
reminded him.

"Well, I've been trying to get you to go out with
me for weeks, I figured if we had an extra friend
maybe you'd reconsider."

"I've got to get back to my class," Claire said
shutting him down and turning to Faith, "Mrs.
Williams, I can give you a call after school and let you
know how Hannah's first day went."

"Yes, of course, Miss Hebert. Thank you so
much." Faith played along, then hurried down the
hallway. In true Dale form, he just stood openly
admiring Faith's retreating figure.

"Ah-hm," Claire cleared her throat to get his
attention. "Don't you have a class to get to, too."

"Ah, yeah. See you, Claire." He started to turn
away then added, "I'm not giving up yet."

Evan cursed at the sound of Squirts voice coming
over his radio yet again. The disgruntled dispatcher
had been messing with him all morning. Apparently
he hadn't gotten over the insult and was looking for
any opportunity to get Evan into trouble. Evan,
knowing how Squirts worked, had been walking the

line. Squirts had obviously decided to content himself with throwing every dog joke he could find at Evan. Torn between turning his radio off to quiet Squirts and getting into trouble for having it off, Evan compromised by turning it down as he watched the highway from his favorite hiding spot. As it had so often lately, his mind turned to Claire.

Evan couldn't believe he had grabbed her that way. Had he been without a woman for that long that he was so desperate? Not that he regretted kissing her. On the contrary, he had enjoyed the kiss a little too much and was looking forward to doing it again. He could still feel the softness of her as she had wrapped herself around him in answer to his kiss.

Evan shook his head to clear it. A car passed on the highway in front of him. He realized Claire had invaded his thoughts again. Not just invaded but conquered. He didn't know if he could trust himself around her. He usually had a little more finesse and a lot more control when it came to women. If his mother knew about this she'd be mortified, or worse she'd be planning a wedding. His wedding. He groaned as his phone rang.

"Yeah," he growled into the phone when he saw his sister's name on the screen.

"So, what's up?" she asked cheerily.

"Working."

"Oh, I thought maybe we could meet up for lunch. The kids are in school. Hannah's in Claire's class."

Ugh. She had talked to Claire. Just what he needed, his sister meddling in his affairs. Surely she would spill the beans to their mother. It was only a matter of time.

"Oh, yeah, um... I think I'll have to take a rain

check, Sis."

"Oh. ok."

Evan heard the disappointment in her voice and felt guilty, but the last thing he needed was his sister grilling him for information. Information he really didn't have. He couldn't have explained his actions if he tried. But maybe, he was reading too much into it. They hadn't had much time to talk without the kids around. Maybe she just needed someone to talk to.

"Well, don't you think it's great that Claire is Hannah's teacher and she lives next door. I really like her, don't you?"

Someone to talk to, my ass, Evan thought to himself. She was trying to play innocent, but he knew she was fishing for information.

"Yeah, she's nice. She's probably a great teacher, too. Look, we'll have lunch later in the week, ok? I've got some calls I need to check on," he lied.

He had been driving all morning trying to get his mind off of Claire. It didn't help that he hadn't gotten much sleep. Most of his night was spent tossing and turning. When he did finally fall asleep he had the most erotic dream of his life starring none other than the curvy little school teacher sporting that damn dress. In his dream, the dress had glowed and shimmered. The swirling colors of the dress had seemed to be moving around her, caressing her body in all the places he wanted his hands. Her laugh had echoed around him as he reached for her.

"Evan? You still there?" His sister's voice brought him back to the present and he groaned.

"Yeah," he said as he adjusted himself in the seat.

"Tomorrow?" she asked hopefully.

"I'll give you a call if I'm not busy. Gotta go." He

clicked the end button.

As soon as the final bell of the day rang, Claire dug her cell phone out of her purse and texted Serena. **"coming over bringing food."**

She had been distracted all day. She was so unsure of herself. It had taken her a long time to be ok with the person she was. Suddenly, she found herself needing someone else's approval. Well, maybe not approval, but definitely advice. She had found happiness within herself. She didn't need a man to feel like she was worthy, or normal. Then why was she so worried of what Evan thought or wanted. She needed her friend to tell her everything was ok. Or at least listen while she talked herself through her own insecurities and help her eat her weight in pizza.

Claire went home and let Rosie out while she changed and called in the pizza order. Hearing Rosie barking, she looked out the window to see Faith making her way across the yard. Claire met her at the door.

"Hey, I was waiting for you to get home. Did he call you?"

"No, why? Did he say something to you?" Claire asked anxiously.

"No, I tried to get him to have lunch with me, but when I mentioned your name he clammed up."

"Oh, what do you think that means?"

"I don't know. I think he just didn't want to discuss it with me. Why don't we get something to eat? I need to get out the house."

"Um, well, I have plans."

"*Oh God*, please don't tell me you are going out with Dale. I knew I shouldn't have left in such a hurry."

Claire had to giggle at the horrified expression on Faith's face. "No, No. I'm not that desperate. I'm going out to Serena's and bringing pizza. How about you come along?"

"I don't want to invite myself. I just thought maybe we could finish our convo about my brother making out with you."

"Yes, that's definitely a topic of discussion, Mrs. Williams," Claire said in her best schoolmarm voice as she linked her arm through Faith's, "and your insight would be invaluable. Please come along."

"Ok, hang on, let me go tell Mom." Faith's dark ponytail bobbed as she jumped in excitement then practically skipped across the yard.

The ride to Serena's house always made Claire smile. It was a scenic drive and watching Rosie hang her head out the window always warmed her heart. She used the time to fill Faith in about Serena and the house.

The house. It was magnificent. Built sometime in the early 1900's, Serena had called it Colonial Revival. The four massive columns in the front stood proudly as with most of the architecture of the time. Wanting to restore its elegance Serena had it repainted classic white. The porch wrapped around the house with railings that matched the impressive balcony. It needed work, true, but looking at it made Claire feel like she could see what it had been in the past. Serena had instantly fell in love with it. She talked about how she could feel it. Claire liked to think she understood what her friend meant but knew what was between her and the house went way deeper than what she could imagine.

Faith seemed equally excited to meet Serena and to see the house after so many years. Apparently it had been something of a local legend when they were growing up. There were stories about ghosts that roamed through the house but what Claire had gathered from the stories is that the isolated surroundings made it an ideal hangout for young lovers and teens trying to scare their friends.

Serena met them out on the expansive front porch that ran the length of the house. Claire supposed it would have been called the veranda back in the day. She could picture them sitting in wicker chairs sipping iced tea.

"Hope you don't mind. I brought along the new friend I was telling you about. I'm trying to get her to come with me to your class tomorrow night. This is Faith."

"Ah, yes, the sister." Serena smiled warmly. "Welcome to my home."

Claire could tell by Faith's face she was just as overwhelmed by the house as she herself had been the first time she had crossed the threshold.

"Thanks for letting me tag along." She took a long look around her. "How do you stay here all alone? This place is so huge it would creep me out to be here by myself."

Serena's laugh echoed through the entryway and seemed to float up the stairway. "I felt at home here as soon as I saw it. Before even. I dreamed of this house before I came to Cypress Point."

"Claire said you plan on making it a Bed and Breakfast?"

"That's the plan. It's taking a bit longer than I had

hoped, but I'm making progress. Come to the kitchen. I have wine waiting."

They followed her to the back of the house to what clearly was a totally remodeled kitchen. It had a huge farm sink and an island large enough to work on or eat at. Shelves held cookbooks and pots. One side of the room opened into a sun room filled with potted plants. Faith sighed dreamily.

"I know. Isn't it amazing? I love this kitchen. It makes me want to cook something," Claire said.

"Yes, I want to bake something right now." Faith looked around wild eyed.

"Bake away, but somebody better give me the scoop. Now. I know something happened," Serena said pointing a finger at Claire.

Claire immediately started to blush. "Apparently that dress you helped me pick out worked."

"He asked you out?" Serena asked through a brilliant smile.

"Not exactly." Claire sighed.

"Then what exactly?" Serena needled.

"We were talking then suddenly he was kissing me. He said something about my dress, and that we couldn't be friends. I'm not sure. It happened so fast my head was spinning. Then he was gone."

"Well, you definitely have his attention. I knew he had the hots for you," Serena said smugly.

"So what should I do?"

"Pass the pizza. I'll pour the wine," Serena said as she put a glass out for each of them.

Once they were seated with slices of pizza and full glasses of wine. Claire asked again. "What do I do now? Do I call him or should I wait for him to call me? God, I feel like a teenager again."

"We should all be so lucky," Serena commented as she considered. "Hmm, Faith, he's your brother. Is he into making the first move or bold girls?"

Faith nearly spit out her wine. "I don't know. I haven't paid attention to who he dated. There's never been anyone he's been serious about that I know of. Of course, I haven't been around much. But Mom would have said."

"Well, technically he made the first move yesterday," Claire reminded them.

"That's true," Faith agreed.

"I have an idea. Let me do a reading for you," Serena suggested.

"Reading?" Faith asked curiously.

"Yeah, a card reading. I need to practice for the Halloween booth anyway."

"Ooohh, this is so cool," Faith tried to talk with a mouth full of pizza, "Can I watch?"

"Only if it's ok with Claire."

"Um, I guess so. I never did anything like this before."

"Finish up and let's go into the parlor."

The dimly lit parlor was tastefully decorated with a bohemian flair that Claire had come to associate with Serena. Rich jewel tones and bright colors mixed in plush and silk fabrics against the warm wood made the room inviting. Just like Serena, there was nothing rigid or formal here.

"Now have a seat," she said as she lit a candle on the table in between them. She pulled another chair from against the wall up to the table for Faith.

"This is normally a private thing." She looked into Claire's eyes. "Are you sure this is ok with you?"

"Yes. Let's do this."

The air became still as Serena pulled a worn deck of tarot cards from a velvet bag and began to shuffle. She handed the deck to Claire and told her to cut into three piles. Faith watched wide eyed on the edge of her seat.

Serena picked up the piles and began to lay out the cards. She sucked in her breath and let it out in a soft gasp. The strange pictures had no meaning to Claire. She looked at them hoping for some clue to what her future held.

"What does it say?"

"You've made a good start. New friends and opportunities."

"Yes. That's the truth."

"You'll have a choice to make soon. Someone from your past will contact you...," she hesitated, "It won't be a happy reunion." Claire gulped loudly. Serena glanced over at Faith then put a hand on Claire's arm.

"Should we just forget about this?" she asked softly.

"No. What about Evan? Does it say anything about that?"

"I think that's the choice. He's here," she said pointing out a card then moving to the next. "And this card represents the chance for a sudden and passionate love affair. There's obstacles, but you mustn't give up."

"So I should go for it?" Claire blue eyes twinkled mischievously.

"Well, that's up to you," Serena said as she picked up the cards.

"Yes! Just do it!" Faith cheered and held up her

wine glass. "This calls for more wine, and brownies."

"Brownies? Did you bring brownies?"

"No, I didn't but if Serena has the ingredients I'll make some."

Serena laughed. "I'll go check my pantry. I don't know if I have everything you need." She headed back to the kitchen. Claire grinned from ear to ear as they got up to follow Serena.

"There's that blush again," Faith teased Claire as they passed a mirror in the foyer. Claire stopped to look at herself.

"I can't help it. I guess I'm just a hopeless romantic."

"It's ok. I think deep down we all are. No matter how much we've been hurt, we want to believe in the fairy tale." Faith smiled sadly into the mirror. Claire started to tell her that she would find someone else when Faith turned and looked upstairs.

"What's wrong?"

"Did you hear that?"

"No. What?"

"Nothing. I thought I heard something but I must've been wrong. Let's go find Serena." Faith said as she pushed Claire towards the kitchen.

CHAPTER 10

You can do this. He kissed you, remember?
Claire had been giving herself a pep talk ever since she had decided to go for it with Evan. Serena and Faith seemed to think she was doing the right thing and she hadn't heard from Evan since the kiss. Faith said he'd been avoiding her, saying he was busy with work.

Claire had decided to buy a big bag of dog food to donate to his shelter in case she lost her nerve. It gave her an excuse for showing up at his house uninvited. If he had changed his mind about her, it wouldn't be so embarrassing for either of them. That's what she was telling herself anyway. She had been a nervous wreck all day at school, even her students had noticed. She had made it through belly dancing class on auto pilot. Her mind wandered as she moved with the music only to be interrupted by Faith asking her what she planned to do about Evan. She didn't have a plan. She figured once she got there it would just happen.

The butterflies in her stomach weren't calmed by the figure eights. Now, driving up his driveway, they were in full revolt. She clutched the steering wheel and took a deep breath. *Maybe he's not home.* She almost wished he wouldn't be there. *What had she been thinking? This was insane. If he had wanted to see her he would have showed up before now. It had only been two days, maybe he had been busy.*

Suck it up! she scolded herself. *If you leave now you are worse than a chicken and you damn well know you won't be able to sleep at all tonight.*

The chorus of barking dogs interrupted her thoughts. She realized she was just sitting there in her car arguing with herself. The ruckus had brought Evan out of the house, freshly showered and wearing only basketball shorts. Before she could turn off the engine he was making his way to her car.

"Hey there."

"Hi! I brought some dog food," she started then realized how awkward it sounded. She felt her face flush.

He gave her a smirk and said, "Ok, let me get it for you. Trunk or back seat?"

"Um," her mouth was suddenly dry. "The back seat," she stammered. He opened the car door and hefted the bag over his shoulder.

"Come on in. I was just fixing me something to eat."

Claire wasn't sure she should intrude, but followed him to the house anyway. Admiring the way his taunt back muscles rippled as he set the bag of food on the porch, she remembered to close her mouth before he turned to hold the door open for her. The aroma from the kitchen made her stomach growl. She hadn't been able to eat anything earlier. Her nerves wouldn't let her. She hoped he wouldn't notice.

"Hungry?" he asked.

"Um, no not really. I didn't mean to interrupt your supper."

"You're not interrupting anything, and I have plenty to share. How about a beer?" he offered.

"Ok."

Evan could see how nervous she was. When he had seen her sitting in her car, it seemed obvious she was struggling with her decision to be here. He had watched curiously half expecting her to back out the driveway, but then she had noticed him. He was surprised and pleased to find her in his driveway. He had been struggling himself. Wrestling with the decision to call her, go see her or just leave it alone. He had almost decided that was the smartest option. Just let it go and pretend nothing happened between them. Watching her now as she fidgeted with the hem of her blouse and looking around nervously, he was glad she had made the decision for him. It occurred to him that she was obviously still struggling, so he tried to put her at ease.

He told her to have seat, and went to get the beers from the kitchen. That's what he'd do, ask her about her class, feed her some of the roast he'd been slow cooking all day and get her to relax.

Claire sat on the sofa, then stood back up. She should just leave. No, he invited you in and offered you a beer. He wants you here. He could have just taken the dog food and said, *"Thanks, see ya' around."* She took a deep breath and willed the butterflies to stop.

"Claire? Are you ok?" Evan asked as he put the beers down on the coffee table.

"Yes," she barely squeaked then found her voice. "Yeah, I'm fine."

"Are you sure? Hey, I promise I don't bite. It's ok." He said softly his voice filled with concern.

"I've been wondering about something."

"Ok?" He eyed her curiously as she took a few steps closer to him.

"There's something I need to know."

"What?"

She pulled his head down to hers and kissed him full on the mouth. He groaned and wrapped his arms around her pulling her close. She was drowning again. The butterflies were replaced with a warm longing that spread out through her body. He broke the kiss with a growl.

"If that's a question the answer is definitely yes," Evan murmured into her ear.

"No, I wanted to make sure it wasn't just the dress you liked," she said in a whisper looking up at him with those big blue eyes filled with uncertainty and longing.

"Oh hell. Let me see if I can clear that up for you."

He kissed her again, long and slow, then trailed kisses down her neck as his hands busily unhooked her bra under her shirt. She moaned as his big warm hands found her heavy aching breasts releasing another wave of raw desire.

Claire knew it had been a long time since a man had touched her, but she never remembered feeling this overwhelming need. She ran her hands over his back reveling in the feel of his hands upon her. To her dismay, she was suddenly standing in front of him completely naked and utterly alive.

"What dress?" he asked as he pulled her down to the carpet.

CHAPTER 11

Claire floated through the last two days with a smile plastered on her face. To say that she was giddy was definitely an understatement. She melted inside every time she thought of Evan. Needless to say, she was in a constant state of gooeyness. It was Friday and he had asked her out to dinner. The only dark cloud had been a call from her mother last night. Well, actually it had been good to hear her mother's voice, but some of her mother's news was disturbing. She had gotten a few calls from Richie. After all this time, she didn't understand why was he bothering her mother. In the voice mails he had left, he sounded pleasant and had politely asked after Claire. She wasn't sure what to think of that, but she was hoping that Serena would be able to shed some light. The card reading hinted about someone from her past. If it was just a few phone calls to her mother she could handle that. Debra was hoping he'd move on and Claire would never hear from him again. *Ignore the problem and it'll go away.* That was Debra's motto. In this case, Claire hoped her mother was right and that Serena would agree. She was on her way there now.

She had called an emergency I-don't-know-what-to-wear meeting of her friends. Both Serena and Faith were expecting details. Claire blushed at the thought of trying to explain what had happened between her and Evan. She could honestly say that it had never been like that with anyone else. It was like someone had cast a magic spell on them.

Claire sighed as she drove up to Serena's house. Faith had said she would meet her here but her car was not in the driveway. She parked her car and grabbed her few choices of clothing to show to her friends. Serena must have been waiting for her because the door opened before she had a chance to knock.

"Hey, I'm so excited for you. Where's Faith?" Serena asked looking behind Claire.

"I don't know. She said she'd meet me here. I didn't see her car when I went home to let Rosie out and grab my clothes." She looked down at the few garments on her hands and frowned. "All of my clothes are teacher clothes, except for that dress and he's already seen me in that."

"Don't worry about that, come on in. We'll fix you up." She followed Serena into the house and back to the kitchen.

"I wanted to ask you about the card reading. Remember you said something about someone from my past coming back."

"Yeah?"

"Richie called my mom," Claire said as she plopped down on a stool at the island counter.

"Why would he call your mom?"

"Well, I think he wants to see to me. I didn't exactly leave a forwarding address if you know what I mean. My mom hasn't actually spoken to him. He left a few messages for her. She says he was very polite, but she doesn't trust him. She's hoping he doesn't call back. I was just wondering if that is what the cards meant."

"Well it could be, but I don't know," Serena said hesitantly, "Maybe we should do another reading."

A knock at the door made them both jump.

"That must be Faith. I wonder where she's been." Serena started out of the room to answer the door.

"Hey, don't say anything to her about Richie. I don't want to discuss that nightmare. It's so embarrassing."

"Ok, but we will talk about it later. I don't think he'll give up that easily, and the cards said a reunion, an unhappy one at that." Serena shook a finger at Claire then went to let Faith in.

Claire had left during one of Richie's walkabouts. Well, that's what she called them. It had sounded so much better than the reality of it. He would disappear with his friends for days. She could only imagine what they were up to. At first she couldn't help but worry, but by the end of their relationship she would look forward to the break away from his constant bullying. She hoped he would just forget about her and not come back. He always did. After that last trip to the ER, she knew she had to get out before she couldn't. It was as simple as that. She started saving her money, and packing away things she didn't need. A friend from her old job had offered her a place to stay. She would bring packed boxes a few at a time to the new place. The next time he left, she got her friends to help move her furniture out to the new place and she just never went back. A few weeks had passed without a word and she began to breathe easier, but was never able to fully relax. That's when she decided to get a dog. Her mom had wanted her to get a guard dog, something to protect her. She looked around at different breeds and decided she wanted a large dog. The problem was she realized she was afraid of the more aggressive breeds. She remembered seeing Rosie for the first time. Just one look at that goofy little black and white puppy had melted her heart. She knew she needed Rosie just as much as Rosie needed her. No, she wasn't exactly a guard dog, but she was a great companion.

Claire still had been nervous that Richie would show up, so she decided to look for another job in a different location. The opening in Cypress Point had been exactly what she needed. It had been scary, but she had promised herself things would be different in this place. It was different. She had gotten her confidence back, had a new job, new friends, and the beginning of a new relationship that promised to be something amazing. Could Richie ruin that for her? She felt sick to her stomach.

No, she wouldn't let him. She had come this far and was happy. He was old news. The familiar song popped into her head. *Yesterday's gone. Don't you look back.* She turned to her friends as they came into the kitchen.

"You have got to spill it now, Claire. I have been waiting for days. My brother has been too busy to get the scoop from and something tells me he wouldn't be so eager to talk to me anyway."

"We waited for you, Faith. Where were you anyway?" Serena asked from behind her.

"Oh, that's not important. Don't change the subject. Details," Faith demanded as she sat next to Claire.

"God, I was so nervous driving up there. I was arguing with myself the whole way."

"But you went, right?"

"Oh yeah, before I knew it I was sitting in his driveway, and there he was standing on the porch looking at me." She ran a hand over her face. "No telling how long I had been sitting there. He came and got the dog food out of the car for me."

"Dog food?" her friends asked in unison.

"Oh, I figured I'd donate dog food, and that gave me a reason to be there. You know, in case I was reading this whole thing wrong." Both of her friends were just looking at her.

"What? Was that stupid?"

"Honestly, hun. Dog food was a nice gesture and I'm sure it's appreciated but there's no mistaking he's got the hots for you. That's just silly," Serena said patting her hand.

Claire grinned. "Yeah I guess so." She could feel herself blushing again.

"Then what?" Serena prompted.

"Well, he invited me in and offered me food. I was still so nervous I didn't know what else to do, so I kissed him." Hoots of laughter erupted from Serena and Faith.

"I would have loved to be a fly on the wall for that!" Faith exclaimed.

"Well, I'm glad you weren't. Look, that's all I'm saying besides it was completely wonderful. He asked me out to dinner tonight, and I've been walking on air since. I need you guys to help me figure out what to wear."

"Girl, I don't think it would matter. I've seen the way he looks at you. You could wear a flour sack and the end result would be the same." Faith wiggled her eyebrows at Claire.

"What does that mean?" Claire asked innocently.

"He's gonna end up taking it off of you at some point," Faith clarified.

"You do realize we are talking about your brother, right?"

"Yes, and I am going to love every minute of ragging him about it, too. I feel like we're back in high school, except this time it's not him sticking his nose in my business. The black skirt is good, you can always dress that up." Faith held up the skirt.

"He was nosey?" Claire couldn't help but giggle.

"Well, let's just say he played the big brother part a little too well. And don't forget he is a cop. They are nosey by nature, I guess."

Claire realized Serena had gotten very quiet. She was standing at the sink just gazing out the window.

"Serena, what's wrong?"

"Hmmm, oh, nothing. I was just thinking about something."

"You looked pretty serious there. You sure everything's ok?"

"I'm sure. I think the skirt is a great idea. I may have something in my closet to go with it if you want something less teacher-ish." She raised an eyebrow at Claire. "I'm making coffee if anybody wants some."

"Sure, let's go look in her closet," Faith hopped off the stool and headed toward the service stairs then stopped. "Where's the bedroom? Is it up here?" she asked motioning to the stairs.

"No, it's down here for now. I'm still working on the upstairs' rooms."

"Ok, good. This big old house still creeps me out. If I had to go upstairs someone would definitely have to come with me." She peeked up into the dark stairwell.

"What are you afraid of?" Serena asked coming up behind her.

"I don't know. You know there's stories of this place being haunted, right?"

"So I've heard."

"That doesn't bother you?"

"No, I'm more afraid of real live people than dead ones."

"So you've never experienced anything?"

Serena considered for a moment then sighed. "Yes, not often, but doors open and shut and I hear footsteps."

Faith's eyes grew huge and she swallowed loudly then asked, "Have you ever heard crying?"

"Crying? That's a new one."

"I've never heard anything." Claire started to pout then looked at Faith. "Oh my God. Faith, is that what you heard last time we were here?" Claire blurted out.

"You heard crying? Why didn't you say something?"

"I wasn't sure, and Claire didn't hear it so it couldn't have been. Let's just stop. I'm freaking myself out."

Serena grabbed Faith by the shoulders and turned her around towards the hallway.

"It's through the parlor we were in the other day. I

left the door open. You'll see it."

"I don't remember seeing a door."

"The bookcase is a door," Claire explained.

"Oh wow. That's so Scooby Doo!" Her dark eyes shone with excitement for a moment then her face grew serious as she asked, "How did you find it?"

"It wasn't always there. I had it put in. I figured it would make a neat conversation piece and a good way to hide the home office." Serena grinned.

"You are just loving this, aren't you? I'm jealous. I hope I find something to be this passionate about."

"You will. Let's get Claire dressed then maybe I can do a reading for you."

"Really? Um, well I guess." Faith tried to shrug off her excitement. As soon as Faith left the room, Claire turned to Serena.

"What's wrong? And don't tell me it's nothing."

Serena sighed. "Look just be careful, ok. The Richie thing is making me nervous. I think it was worse than what you've told me and if that's the case you should be worried too."

A muffled "This is so cool!" sounded from the parlor as Faith found the secret doorway.

"I shouldn't have told you. I don't want you to worry." Claire shook her head.

"Just now, I remembered a dream I had. Faith's crack about the flour sack. I dreamed this..," Serena said sweeping her arms out for emphasis.

"Like a déjà vu?" Claire's eyes widened.

"No, it was a dream. We were here looking at dresses. They were white dresses and we were all picking them out. You were supposed to go first, then Faith, then me. That was the order we were to be married in."

"Oh wow, I like this dream…," Claire said excitedly. Serena shook her head slowly.

"No. Then it got dark and you were crying. There was blood on your dress and I couldn't find you."

"But it was just a dream," Claire said rubbing the gooseflesh that had appeared on her arms.

"Look, you don't understand. Some of my dreams are foreshadowings. Mostly symbolic, but they come true."

"Hey, I might have to borrow this for myself. I absolutely love it." Faith came in holding up several shirts. The look on Claire and Serena's faces made her stop. "What's going to come true?"

"Oh, it was just a silly dream Serena had."

"Not silly," Serena snapped.

"What was it?" Faith asked curiously.

"She dreamed we were picking out wedding gowns for each of us," Claire said trying to lighten the mood.

"Oh, well, if it's all the same to you guys, I'll pass on that. I'll be there for both of you, but I've been down that road and I'm not doing that again," Faith said rolling her eyes.

"We'll see about that. Just remember I told you so." Serena smirked. "Now let me see, what you've got there. Were you shopping for you or Claire?" she teased.

"Both. Not that I have a social life or anything, but I do need to find a job. By the way, how's the fortune telling booth coming along?"

"Serena has gone a bit overboard, but I think it's going to be a hit."

"Hey, while I'm thinking about it, we need a small table for our booth. All the ones I have are pretty heavy and won't fit in my car. It would be hard to move them."

"Hmm, I have that small round side table."

"The one in your living room? It's like the perfect size," Serena said excitedly.

"It's nothing fancy. I picked it up at a flea market when I first moved away."

"If you don't mind us using it for the booth that would be great. We'll cover it with the table cloth."

"Not a problem. I feel like you've done more than your share."

"Bring it by tomorrow. I want to see it all set up. I've got the frame ready. I just want to make sure the curtains will look right."

"Sure, and maybe you can tell me what I'm going to be doing exactly. We've less than two weeks."

"Yeah, I'll give you some pointers. I'm sure we'll be busy."

"I'd offer to help but I've got to take the kids around," Faith said apologetically.

"That's ok. Just make sure to bring the kids by to see us. I enjoy seeing them dressed in costumes," Claire said rubbing her hands over a silky plum colored draped neck blouse. "I love this one."

"Go try it on. With the skirt. I've got some killer heels that would go with that, if you can fit in them."

"I don't even know where we're going. That might be a bit much don't you think?"

"My brother better not even think about taking you to the diner here in town. He'd better take you somewhere fancy," Faith demanded.

"Hello? Where you are going is not the point. Last time I picked out an outfit for you, he seemed to like it," Serena reminded her.

Claire blushed remembering just how much he

liked it, and how sweet he was when he had promised her that it wasn't just about the dress. Then proceeded to show her. She jumped up from her perch on the stool and hurried to try it on.

CHAPTER 12

 Evan couldn't believe how nervous he was as he drove to pick up Claire for their date. He had no reason to be this nervous. Hell, they had already slept together.

He hadn't been this nervous on his first date and that hadn't turned out too well for him. He had been in love, or what he thought at the time to be love. Tracey McMillian. God, he would have sworn the sun set and rose just for her. He could still recall the way the sun had made her blond hair shine as she cheered on the sidelines. He had finally worked up the nerve to ask her out after football practice. Her blue eyes had sparkled as she gave him a sidelong glance then agreed to the date. He had bought her flowers. He laughed at himself thinking back. In his nervousness he had handled the flowers so much they were drooping by the time he got to her door. He had it all worked out in his head. They would be sweethearts through high school then the wedding right after graduation. It would be perfect. Little did he know, he wasn't the only football player that had fantasies about Tracey and her pompoms. If the rumors were true, more than one had made that fantasy a reality.

He hadn't believed the stories at first. After dating for all of two weeks, she had moved on to the next football player. He had pushed his broken heart and hurt pride aside, only dating for fun after that. No more thoughts of marriage or forever. Date a girl for a while, if she seemed to get too attached, he'd find a new one. He had to admit it had been a lot more fun that way.

Now at his age, it seemed to him, sweaty palms and butterflies were just plain ridiculous. Unless, it was some sort of medical condition. Hell, maybe he should make an appointment with old Doc Miller just to be on the safe side he thought as drove up to Claire's house.

Thankfully no one was outside at his parents' house next door. He had been avoiding Faith all week. He just wasn't ready to discuss his relationship or whatever this thing was with his nosey sister. It was inevitable and there would be no stopping the jokes and teasing. He knew it was coming. He just wanted to put it off as long as he could.

When Claire answered the door, the sight that greeted him had him grabbing for his chest. Damn, maybe he would make that appointment. She smiled up at him and the tightening was no longer in his chest but coming from down in his jeans. He should have brought her flowers, or candy. Or both.

"Shit."

"Well, hello to you too."

"Ah, sorry." He gave her a quick peck on the cheek. "What I meant to say was, you look great. Are you ready to go?"

He was really hoping she wouldn't invite him in. There's no way he would be able to keep his hands off of her. Claire's hair was fixed different. It was pulled up in the back in some kind of swirl. He didn't know what that style was called but he was liking it. It drew his gaze to the purple stone baubles dangling from her ears, to her neck then down to the cleavage that was peeking out above the folds of silky fabric.

"Yeah, let's just go. I'm having a hard time keeping Rosie's hair off of my skirt. I'd hate for you to be covered in it too," she said motioning to his jeans then turned to lock her door. "I hope I'm not overdressed."

"Darlin', don't worry about that. I'd have to be a stupid man to not want to show you off," he said as he walked her to his truck and opened the passenger door.

Climbing in was a bit of a challenge in those crazy heels Serena had talked her into wearing. Evan had to give her a little boost to help her up. It gave him a chance to admire how well the skirt fit snuggly to her rear. She was thankful when she landed in the seat without splitting her skirt. It was one of her favorite skirts, but obviously not made for climbing into big macho trucks.

Once Evan had settled into his seat and started to back out of the driveway, Claire was struck with a bout of nervousness.

"So where exactly are we going?"

"Well, I thought since you haven't been here that long, you probably haven't had a chance to go out exploring."

"I've been out of town a few times with Serena, shopping in Lafayette. I hadn't been there in years. I was shocked how much it's grown."

"That's right. Mom did say that you moved from

Texas but you were originally from Louisiana. What made you move back?"

"I didn't like living in the city," she said easily. It wasn't a lie.

"Well, I guess you like Cypress Point then." He laughed.

"Yes, I do. Have you ever lived anywhere else?"

"Just for a while after high school. Then I decided to go into law enforcement. Got a job with the Sheriff's office so I could stay close to my parents."

"Really?"

"Yeah, well, when Faith graduated she went off to LSU. I didn't like the idea of not being around for them. Our younger sister, Elle, was quite a handful."

"That's nice, but didn't you ever want to just move away and start over where no one knew you?"

"Why?" He seemed perplexed at her question. Not willing to give too many details of her own past she decided to ignore his inquiry.

"You never said where we were going." She said trying to change the subject back to something safe. Evan took the hint and shrugged it off.

"Have you ever heard of Pont Breaux in Breaux Bridge?"

"No, I don't think so."

"It's a nice place, great food, and music. Do you like to dance?"

"Yes. Well, it's been a while, but yes. I don't go out much since I got Rosie. I hate to leave her alone for too long."

The restaurant surprised her. She wasn't sure what she was expecting, but it brought back so many memories of growing up in a small Louisiana town.

The smells of the food cooking mixed with the sounds of the live Cajun band almost had her tearing up. She hadn't realized how much she had missed these simple but joyful things. People coming together to enjoy good food and music. Music that made you want to dance.

The building itself was not a grand structure, but the vehicles parked in front spoke of its popularity. Amid the tables covered in red and white checkered cloths stood the focal point, a small bandstand backed with a mural of Louisiana scenery and a wooden dance floor lined with real cypress trunk columns.

The menu offerings had Claire's mouth watering as she tried to make a decision on what to order. Finally deciding on the crabmeat au gratin and a small bowl of the seafood gumbo, she relaxed as she listened to the band play.

They passed the time talking about music until the food came. Living out of the area for so long, she didn't know any of the local musicians or bands. Evan mentioned names of the more popular bands that he thought she might be interested in seeing.

The food arrived and the discussion turned to favorite cuisine. Claire savored every bite of the rich cheese and lump crab meat. It took everything she had not to moan with pleasure. Using her fork to scrape up the last bit of cheese from her plate, she looked up to see Evan watching her with an amused look on his face.

"What?"

"Nothing. Was it good?"

"Yes, it was amazing. I'll have to sit here for a while to let it go down."

"Me too, Darlin'." Evan laughed and gave her a

wink. Blushing, Claire put down her fork, and turned her attention to the dance floor.

Watching the older couples glide across the dance floor made her happy. She didn't know why, it just did. She guessed that the dance itself was like life, with the right partner, someone you trusted, it could be a thing of beauty. The longer you were together the easier it became. She looked over at Evan and wondered if they could dance together. Would they glide or trip over each other? Sure, they had gotten off to a rocky start, but you had to learn the steps first, right?

As if reading her mind, he held out his hand.

"Let's give it whirl, huh?"

"Oh yes, let's. It's been a while but I'm willing to try." Claire meant every word. Evan didn't have a clue how badly she wanted to dance, and dance with him.

One song bled into another. By the time they got back to their table, Claire was almost limping. Damn, shoes. She couldn't remember the last time she had this much fun but the fear of maiming her feet permanently had her looking for her chair.

"What's wrong?"

"Nothing." Claire tried to play it off.

"You look like you're in pain. Did you hurt yourself? I know I didn't step on your toes," he teased.

"No." She couldn't help but smile at him. He hadn't stepped on her toes at all. Quite the opposite, he had made her feel graceful and light on her feet. These *killer heels* as Serena had aptly called them were making her feet ache and throb.

"Ah, these shoes. They're pretty but not exactly made for dancing. I'm more of a sensible shoe type person."

He looked down at the shoes and shrugged. "So take 'em off."

"Oh gosh, no." She reached for her water glass and longed to fish out an ice cube to rub over her sore feet.

"Oh, come on. Kick 'em off. Unless you're done. If so, we can call it a night." Evan shrugged and looked back at the dance floor.

She thought about it for all of two seconds then reached down and plucked the torture devices off of her aching feet. Claire stood up and took a step to see if she could still walk. The throbbing was still there, but the shooting pains were gone.

"I think I'm good for another round or two." She smiled at him. He laughed and spun her onto the dance floor then pulled her in close.

"I tell you what, a few more dances then we will get you home. I'll rub your feet, I promise," he said into her ear.

"You've got a deal."

Evan kept his promise. As soon as they were back at her house, he sat down on the sofa and patted the seat next to him.

"Come on over here and let me see your feet."

He had been a true gentleman. When she was trying to cross the parking lot in her bare feet he had scooped her up and carried her to the truck. They did get a few strange looks, but she didn't care. Anything not to put those shoes back on. She had completely ruined the pantyhose but it was well worth it in her opinion.

"Really?" she asked as she wrangled Rosie off of

Evan and towards the kitchen.

"Yes, I promised. I keep my promises. Unless you don't want me to?"

"Far be it for me to make you break a promise. I won't have that on my conscience. Just give me a minute." She let Rosie out the back door then went into the bathroom to get rid of the shredded hosiery. There was nothing sexy about your toes sticking out through the holes in your stocking feet. She giggled to herself as she looked in the mirror on the way out of the bathroom.

After letting Rosie back in, and grabbing a couple of water bottles she headed back to the sofa and her foot rub. Claire sighed as she plopped down and swung her feet up on his lap. His big warm hands felt so good on her throbbing foot. First one then the other. She was having a hard time concentrating on what he was saying.

"Mmmm, what?"

"I asked if you had plans for tomorrow," he said laughing.

"Kind of. Why?"

"It's no big deal. I have to take one of the strays to the Acadiana Shelter. Hopefully to meet his new owner. I just thought you could ride along and we could get a bite to eat somewhere along the way."

"That sounds nice, but I've already promised Serena we'd work on our booth for the Halloween festival. We've got to set up and do like a dress rehearsal."

"Far be it for me to make you break a promise." He mimicked her earlier response and started to tickle the underside of her feet. Claire tried to pull her feet away. He grabbed her legs and pulled her closer. The unexpected movement brought back a flood of memories. Frozen by unwelcome flashes of Richie's face twisted in anger and those cold calculating eyes, Claire held her breath without realizing it.

In that one movement, Evan had slid himself over her. She looked into those dark eyes and found no anger or malice, only desire. Flashes of Richie were instantly replaced with the memories of Evan, gentle and passionate. She exhaled with a soft gasp.

"That's ok. Maybe next time." He smiled down at her. "Did I tell you how much I like your hair like that?"

She giggled. "My hair?"

"Yep. It's pretty and shows off your neck." He planted a trail of soft kisses up the side of her neck. "But you want to know my favorite thing about it?" he asked as he pulled gently on her earring with his teeth.

"What?" she asked breathlessly.

"This." He reached up and shook the pins out freeing her hair. "I've been wanting to do that since you opened the door."

"Want to know what I've been wanting since I opened the door?"

"What?"

"For you to kiss me."

"I figured I'd wait for you to kiss me when you were ready. That worked out pretty well for me last time." He gave her a sly smile.

"So you weren't going to kiss me unless I kissed you first?"

"Well, I'm running out of patience, so I hope you plan to kiss me soon," he teased.

She lifted her head until their lips were almost

touching. The electricity between them was palpable. Claire felt a spark as she traced his lips with her tongue. One hand still tangled in her hair, Evan groaned and pulled her head to his.

"Close enough for me, Darlin'," he mumbled as his mouth found hers. Claire wrapped her arms around him and deepened the kiss. *This has to be magic,* she thought to herself as she ran her hands up and down his back. His free hand caressed her side and slid down to cup her butt. She felt like they were floating together on some wave. She wanted to wrap herself around him but found it hard to move in her tight skirt. Evan had found his way under her blouse. She pulled away from the kiss and put a hand on his chest.

"What? Am I hurting you?" His voice was full of concern. Her heart melted.

"No, it's just this couch isn't very comfortable. Maybe we should go to the bed."

He smiled at her. "Sounds good to me."

He helped her up off the couch. She grabbed his hand and pulled him down the hall to her bedroom.

There was enough light from the bathroom so she didn't bother turning on the bedroom light. When she reached the bed, she turned to face him. Instead of reaching for him, she unzipped the tight fitting skirt and slid it down her legs.

"I was going to do that, but I like this game," he said as he reached for his belt buckle. His jeans joined her skirt on the floor. "I see your skirt and raise you a shirt."

As he stripped off his shirt, she was stunned by the beauty of him. In the pale light, his body, hard and muscular, almost appeared to glow. This was magic.

Somehow, somewhere he had been so perfectly and wonderfully made just for her in this moment.

She didn't want to ruin it, but there was no way to gracefully get out of Serena's blouse. Apparently she was a bit bigger in the bust area and had struggled to get the silky shirt over her boobs. Once on, it had the desired effect of showing off her cleavage while making her waist seem slimmer. She'd be mortified if she ripped the shirt or worse, if she got stuck in it half off. She imagined it stuck over her head with her arms flailing about. Nope, not sexy. She sighed.

Evan feared she had begun to change her mind. She stood there gazing at him so long, he almost became uncomfortable.

"Well, I might need some help getting out of this shirt. It's kind of tight." She grimaced. He let out a chuckle and reached for her.

"Not a problem. I'm a trained professional."

It wasn't a smooth operation, but it was easier with someone to help peel it over her head. By the time the extraction was complete they were both laughing. Evan pushed her back unto the bed and fell on her.

This time there was nothing to confine her. She wrapped her legs around him loving the feel of him hard against her. She groaned as Evan nipped at her breast through the fabric of her bra.

Rosie padded into the room and stopped.

"Bedtime Rosie," Claire commanded. Rosie went over to her bed in the corner of room and plopped down.

Uncertain of how Rosie would react to having Evan in her bed, Claire flipped a blanket over them. Evan didn't seem to mind. Having freed her breasts he was teasing them with his mouth. Claire moaned and rubbed herself against him. A snort from the edge of the blanket froze them both.

"No Rosie, bedtime." Rosie whined and let out a little woof. Claire giggled.

"Sorry, she thinks we're playing hide and seek. Sometimes I hide under the blanket," Claire explained. "Let me put her in the other room."

Claire got up and brought Rosie back to the living room and commanded her to go to bed. Rosie laid on her bed in the living room and gave Claire a questioning look. Claire knew she must be confused. She had never had a man in her bed since she had taken Rosie home.

As she went back to her room and shut the door behind her, she thought about the dance. This was a different type of dance, but she knew she had the right partner. He made her feel alive and wanted. This time nothing would keep them from finishing this age old dance and she knew it would be enjoyable for both of them.

CHAPTER 13

"What does it mean?" Claire asked as she peered closer to the cards. She had brought the table as requested. It was draped now with a rich burgundy velvet cloth and nestled in the cozy handmade tent. With only the lit candle between them for light, Claire knew they had achieved the atmosphere they were going for.

"Someone from your past will reconnect with you. It's not good. Same as last time." Serena shook her head at the cards laid out before them.

"So, what do I do? Should I call him and get it over with?"

"No, I wouldn't encourage it. I'm still having that dream. I know it has to do with Richie. He's going to hurt you. Stay away from him."

"Will he just go away if I ignore him?" Claire asked hopefully.

"I don't know, but I don't see how contacting him would help either."

"What else does it say? Evan's still in there somewhere, right?"

Serena hesitated before answering. "Yes, but

there's problems there, too."

"No. That can't be right. There's no problems. It's awesome." Claire blushed.

"That's just it." Serena tapped a card. "Temperance reversed."

"Is it bad?" Claire asked in a whisper.

"It's just reminding you not to rush things. There's confusion and frustration, but you can't push things. It has to happen in its own time," Serena tried to explain.

"Well, I don't understand. Last time, it said to go for it, right?"

"Yes, but that was last time, things change constantly. Every action changes things. Do you understand?"

"No," Claire pouted, "but it's saying now to wait?"

"Yes."

"For what? For what's going to happen with Richie or with Evan?" Claire scratched her head.

Serena sighed and started to explain but was interrupted by a voice outside their makeshift tent.

"Anybody home?" Faith stuck her head into one of the openings. "Can I play, too? This is neat."

"Hey, Faith. We were just practicing."

"Great job on the tent. It's beautiful." She ran her hands over the plush colorful fabric of the curtains.

"Thanks. I think it came together nicely."

"Claire, I was looking for you."

"Really?" Claire perked up. "Why?"

"Well, to see how the date went of course," she said grinning at Claire, "...and to invite you to Sunday dinner tomorrow. Mom sent me over to your house but you weren't home. I remembered you mentioned coming over to work on your booth, so I volunteered to come find you. Sorry for crashing the party."

"No problem." She grinned at Faith. "Sunday dinner? Is it like a formal thing?"

"No, it's just Sunday dinner. Mom cooks, we all eat." Faith patted her stomach for emphasis. "Really, no pressure."

"Should I bring something?"

"Nope, just yourself."

Claire looked at Serena. Serena shrugged. "You were invited."

"Ok, I'll be there."

"And the date?"

"Oh, don't get her started again. I'm about sick of hearing her gush about Evan," Serena said rolling her eyes.

"Hey, I thought you were happy for me."

"Oh, I am, hun. I'm just jealous really. I wish I had some hot hunk in my life."

"Ugh, my brother is not a hot hunk, but I take it things went well?"

"Oh yes. We had the best time even though Serena tried to sabotage me with those shoes." Claire gave a menacing glance in Serena's direction.

"They are sexy. You wanted to be sexy remember?"

"Have you ever tried jitterbugging in them?"

"He took you dancing? Aww, that's sweet." Faith plopped in a chair and started to tear up.

"What's wrong?"

"Oh nothing... I think I'm jealous too." She sniffed then looked at the cards on the table. "Now, somebody practice on me. I'm curious as to how this works, and I could use some hope."

"I think I'm beyond hope, it would have to be

magic," Serena said miserably.

"Well, Serena will have to. I'm not sure I understand all of this." Claire shook her head.

"Look over that book I gave you."

"I think I should just stick to giving out the candy. I'm not qualified to read fortunes. It's just for fun anyway."

"Oh, hey, you could hand out fortune cookies too. That would be funny," Faith suggested.

"That's a great idea."

"Did I interrupt your reading? Go ahead and finish with Claire first."

"Oh, we were done." Serena started picking up the cards.

"So who's Richie? Is he the blast from the past that's going to show up?" Faith asked casually.

"Eavesdrop much?" Serena narrowed her dark eyes at Faith.

"It's ok. He's my ex. Emphasis on EX. It ended badly and that's the end of the story."

"That's all I needed to know. My turn."

Serena laughed as she reshuffled the cards. Then handed the deck for Faith to cut. Once the cards were laid out, Serena clucked her tongue a few times and shook her head.

"What? If it's bad. I don't want to hear it." Faith put her hands over her ears.

"Not bad, just... interesting."

"Well, what?" Claire asked leaning over the cards again as if getting closer would help her to understand.

"You've had a great loss. There's betrayal and heartache."

"Well, so far it's on the mark," Faith snorted.

"What else?"

"Good things in the future. On all fronts."

"Like a job?"

"Yes, looks like you'll have a great opportunity to show off your talents."

Faith snorted again. "Whatever that is."

"And it looks like you will be reunited with a childhood friend."

"Well, I am back in my hometown. I saw Tina at the bank."

"No, this is more of the romantic type." Serena closed her eyes and put her hand to her heart. "I'm getting all kinds of sweet feelings."

Faith sat up straight in her chair. "No. That's enough."

"Oh come on, Faith. This is good. Better than mine." Claire pouted.

The friends froze when they heard a door slam overhead followed by sounds of footsteps. Serena looked at her friends. "It's ok. Really. Usually it happens later, but I'm used to it."

Claire held a hand over her mouth as if holding back a scream. Faith had grabbed onto her arm and sat poised as if she was ready to sprint away.

"I know it's scary the first time but really that's it." Serena tried to reassure them.

"Shhhh...." Faith motioned with her free hand to quiet Serena. "Do you hear that?"

A low moan sounded followed by the sound of soft weeping.

"Wow, that's different," Serena whispered in awe as she looked at the ceiling above her. "Is that what you heard before?"

"Yes."

"It sounds like it's directly above us."

"So?"

"Let's go see," Serena said pushing on Faith's arm.

"Are you serious?" Faith asked incredulous. The weeping suddenly stopped and the house grew quiet.

Claire removed her hand from her mouth and took a deep breath. "That was great! It almost made up for that crappy reading."

"Hey. It wasn't crappy," Serena said insulted.

Faith just shook her head at them both. "Did that happen? I'm not crazy."

"No, you're not crazy. We all heard it." Serena patted Faith's arm. "Let's go look around upstairs. Sometimes they move stuff around."

"They?" Faith looked up at the ceiling waiting for more sounds.

Claire jumped up from her chair. "Ok, come on."

"No, I gotta go. Hannah's waiting for me. I told her she could help me make dessert for tomorrow." Faith tried to excuse herself, but Claire wasn't having it.

"Faith, you've got to come with us. Let's go." She grabbed Faith's hand and pulled her out of her chair. Serena led the way up the main staircase to the floor above.

As they made their way up the stairs and onto the spacious second floor landing, evidence of Serena's renovations were obvious. She had been floating and sanding walls in the bedrooms to get them ready to paint, but had not yet made it to the front bedroom where the crying had seemed to be coming from. The room was bare except for a few boxes of Serena's things in the middle of the floor. Claire and Serena walked around the room while Faith stood watching at the doorway.

"It's ok, Faith."

"No, it's not. I don't like it up here." Faith looked behind her nervously.

"Why? I think it's neat. You can practically feel the history." Claire walked to the window and looked out trying to imagine earlier occupants doing the same. A young girl waiting for her lover, a wife awaiting the return of her husband or a worried mother hoping to see her child coming up the drive. This old house had been a home to many throughout the years, the view gradually changing over time. The thought made Claire smile.

"I don't think anything has been moved," Serena said as she examined the boxes then walked to the closet and opened it. The old wooden door creaked as it opened revealing dusty shelves and a pull chain for the empty light fixture.

"I wonder if this is the door I keep hearing," Serena said more to herself than her friends.

"How often does it happen?" Claire asked. Nothing like this had ever happened to her before. She was intrigued.

"Not that often, really. It's been a few weeks. I thought maybe it had something to do with all the changes I've been making to the house, but I don't know."

A flowery fragrance drifted through the air.

"Wow. What is that?" Claire asked as she inhaled the sweet scent.

"It smells like gardenia's, but where's it coming from?" Serena asked as she sniffed the air then looked at Claire. "Do you have on perfume?"

"No," Claire answered shaking her head then suggested, "Air freshener?"

"No. There was no point in bothering with that up here until I finish with the painting."

Claire walked towards the door and the smell started to fade. "Faith, do you smell it?"

"Just barely."

Claire took a few steps toward where Serena was standing at the closet and the smell became stronger. "I think it's coming from the closet."

Serena looked again on the shelves for anything that could be giving off the odor. One by one, she passed her hand over each shelf feeling for anything that could be stuck in the corners.

"I'm too short to reach the top shelves. Faith, can you get my ladder from the other room?"

"Yeah, ok." She looked terrified but went off in search of the ladder. Not even a full minute had passed before she came back hauling the ladder. "Found it."

"Ok, y'all hold it for me. It won't fit inside, so I'm going to have to reach a bit," Serena explained as she set up the ladder as close to the closet opening as possible. She climbed a few steps then reached for a shelf for support. The next step higher had her eye level with the top shelf. Holding on to the side with one hand she reached in and felt around with the other.

"Anything?" Claire asked.

"No, just a lot of dust," Serena answered as she reached farther to feel the back wall. The clack of wood on wood sounded.

"Wait. Something's moving."

"Moving? Like alive?" Faith squeaked.

"No. Like a loose board maybe."

Serena pushed again and the board moved like the top was unattached. She felt for the edges. The top wasn't nailed down and the sides weren't straight but rounded. The bottom of the board was wedged between the shelf and the wall. Using her fingers she pushed and wiggled the odd shaped board inching it slowly upward. After several minutes she managed to get it free. It clattered onto the shelf sending a puff of dust into the air.

Serena coughed waving the dust cloud away. Then grabbing up the board she climbed back down the ladder.

"What is it?"

"I'm not sure. A sign maybe?" One side was flat and the other seemed to be carved. Serena brushed at the surface to clean off the years of dust and dirt. The edges seemed to be carved in a scroll pattern, but the middle was smooth. She rubbed at the dirt harder.

"I think it says something."

"Be careful. It looks old," Faith said peering over her shoulder.

"Maybe we should wash it off," Claire suggested.

"I'm afraid it will take the paint off too."

"Let's try a paint brush. You know, like the archaeologist do." Faith ran from the room to retrieve a brush from the painting supplies in the hallway. She returned holding out a new brush to Serena.

"Hey. Wait." Claire grabbed Serena's arm.

"What?"

"The smell. It's gone."

The three all sniffed at the air around them. Smelling nothing but old wood and dust, Claire walked back to the closet and sniffed again. The flowery scent was gone, replaced with the musty smell of a closed up space.

"No, it's gone."

"Crying and smells. That's interesting," Serena commented as she took the brush from Faith.

"What do you think it means?" Faith asked.

"I don't know but I'd love to figure it out." Serena tried brushing off the wood with soft strokes as her friends watched curiously. Slowly, bit by bit, pieces were uncovered. There had once been gold and black lettering but it was badly faded. Small white flowers were painted around the letters.

"What does it say? I can't make it out."

"I don't think that's English," Claire said trying to make out the lettering.

"It's hard to tell. Some of it's missing. The paint has peeled in some spots."

"Wait. Look here," Faith said pointing. "That looks like a 'you' at the end."

"Yeah, it is," Claire agreed.

"Oh my," Serena said as she brushed at the sign again.

"What?"

"That's bayou. That first fancy letter is a 'B'."

"Something bayou," Faith wondered testing out the name hoping to jog her memory. "Does the bayou back there have a name?"

"I have no idea." Serena shrugged. "I know the river is back there off to one side but I don't know anything about the bayou."

"I'll have to ask my Dad," Faith said looking back down at the sign thinking out loud. "It's got to be old, right? No one's lived here since I can remember. This house is old. So I bet it's French."

Serena looked again, putting down the brush she rubbed her fingers gently over the faded paint.

"I bet you're right. When I bought this house the realtor said the only history they knew was that it was owned by a family that had a plantation. They used the river to export the crops before the railroads came. The plantation went bankrupt or something. A few other families have lived here since then and somewhere along the line they put in electricity and plumbing."

"What do they call this place?" Claire asked excitedly.

"What do you mean? I don't think it has name. It's not one of those big fancy plantations like on the Mississippi."

"No, the night we met. Evan said you lived at the *'something'* place."

"Oh, yeah. We've always called it the old Amie' place. That was the family name of the last people to live here or something, but that was way before my time," Faith recalled nodding in agreement. Claire studied the sign again.

"No, that looks like it's a 'C' not an 'A.'"

"Yeah, that's a 'C' and the rest is kind of hard to make out. Maybe u-r at the end but I'm not certain."

"Heart!" Serena exclaimed.

"No that's a 'C', not an 'H'," Claire said pointing to the fancy script again.

"No, the Cajun word for heart. Spell it."

"I don't speak it and I certainly can't spell it." Claire shook her head.

"Oh. Oh." Faith jumped up and down. "Coeur. C-O-E-U-R"

"You speak French?" Claire looked at Faith in

amazement.

"No, but I do know some words. There's a song my daddy likes and it talks about coeur mal."

Claire gave her a blank look. "You know, broken heart, or sick heart or something to that effect. It's a sad song," Faith tried to explain.

"Oh." Claire shook her head not knowing what else to say. "Is that what it says?"

Serena was staring at the sign. "I'm pretty sure. Coeur du Bayou. Heart of the bayou."

"What's it for?"

"This house. I think it wanted me to know its name."

The friends smiled at each other over the aged plaque as the faint smell of gardenia's floated around them then dissipated.

"I've really got to go. Dessert won't make itself," Faith announced nervously then looked at Claire. "Don't forget about tomorrow."

Claire remembering her invitation smiled and thought about tomorrow. She started humming the familiar song to herself.

CHAPTER 14

Cleaning out the dog kennels wasn't the most pleasant way to start the day, but it was a necessary task and Evan didn't mind. He let the dogs run while he sprayed away the muck. They enjoyed the time by chasing each other and sometimes a stray squirrel. It was quiet for the most part, unless you counted all the barking. Evan enjoyed it because it was another task that gave him time to think. He had done quite a bit of thinking yesterday on his drive to bring the stray to meet the prospective new owners. He wasn't sure what to do about Claire.

Strays were easier. Keep them fed and safe until you find them a good home. At least that had a happy ending. Love at first sight for both parties. He smiled. He loved dogs, true, but even more he loved to see them with people that would love and care for them. Lucky had definitely lucked out. The family that was taking him home would spoil him rotten. No more kennel for him. He would end up sleeping in a bed with their boy. He smiled at the thought.

As he filled the water bowls, he thought of Claire. Again. Is that what he was doing? Taking care of her until he could pass her off to someone who would be there forever. Looking back, he had to admit that seemed to be how his past relationships went. That was something to think about.

He shook his head. *Whoa boy, you barely know her.*

A buzzing from his pocket interrupted his thoughts. He turned off the hose and fished his phone out of his pocket, a text from Faith. **Don't forget Sunday Dinner. Mom's expecting you.** He smiled. It was true his mom would be expecting him, but he was sure his sister was dying to ask him about his date with Claire. Maybe he was paranoid, but he did know his little sister. **I'll be there.** He sent a message back. Hopefully with his parents there he could evade Faith's inquisition.

The smells wafting from the kitchen when he opened the door to his childhood home had his stomach growling. This was still home to him. It would always be. His parents were a constant in his life.

In the brief time he lived away, knowing they were still there if he needed them had been a huge support. Part of why he moved back home was to be there for them in the same way and knowing his mom was cooking was a definite bonus.

"Hey Mom." He smiled as he entered the kitchen and hugged his mom. "Smells great."

"It's just a roast, but it'll be good. I've got some field peas and greens from the garden too."

"And a cake, too? Is it somebody's birthday and I forgot?"

"Faith and Hannah wanted to bake something for dessert. They did a great job. Look how pretty it come out."

"It looks good enough to eat." He caught Hannah as she came in the room and swung her around. "So do you. Where's your brother?"

"He's helping Paw Paw in the shop," she answered in between giggles. Hannah's laughter brought Faith to the kitchen, too.

"Hey Evan. How's it going?" His sister gave him a wicked grin.

"Just fine, little sister. How's it going with you?" He let go of Hannah and she ran back to the living room.

"Great."

"Kids adjusting ok?"

"Oh, yeah, they're fine. They love it here. Already making new friends."

"Good. Heard from the asshole lately?"

"Is that your way of saying *I told you so*?"

"No, just making sure he's not causing any more trouble."

"He calls every now and then to talk to the kids. If it's convenient for him, he may take them for a weekend."

Evan snorted. "Figures. I knew he was a jerk..."

"Shut up, Evan."

"Ok, that is enough." Margaret stepped in. "We know how you feel, it doesn't need to be said." She nodded her head towards the living room where Hannah was watching TV.

Evan caught her meaning and winced. "Sorry. Let's talk about something else."

"Yes, let's, brother dear." Faith grinned at Evan.

"Not that," he said pointing a finger at Faith.

"What?" Margaret asked tipping the lid to check a

simmering pot of rice.

"My love life is none of your concern, little sister."

Faith laughed as she turned to look out the window over the sink. "Well, speak of the devil. Your love life is crossing the yard, or is it the love of your life?" she said with an emphasis on the word love. He walked over to the window to see what Faith was looking at. He put his hands on his sister's shoulders as he came up behind her.

"Why is she coming over here?"

Faith giggled. "Mom told me to invite her to Sunday dinner, since you were busy out of town yesterday." His hands slid around her throat for a gentle squeeze.

"Mom, tell Evan to stop choking me," Faith said teasingly.

"Evan, cut it out. I thought you liked her."

He sighed and leaned back against the counter. "Mom, I like her just fine but I don't think it's to the *'let's have dinner with the parents'* level quite yet.... if ever," he added as he gave his sister a dark look.

"Evan Blaine, she is a sweet girl and my neighbor. If I want to invite her over, I will."

"Mom, I'm just saying we don't know her that well. She might not be as sweet as you think."

"Well, she was sweet enough for some things, Evan, from what I hear."

He groaned. "Shut up Faith. It's none of your business."

"I can't wait till I can say I told you so, brother dear." She stuck her tongue out at him as she headed to the door then turned back to him and winked as she added "at the wedding."

"Wedding?" Margaret squeaked, "Oh Evan. Why

didn't you say something?" His mother was hugging him with tears in her eyes before he could close his mouth.

"Mom, no. No wedding. Faith was joking." He held her away to make sure she heard him. "If I wanted her here, I would have invited her myself, Ok? Just back off. I'm going to find dad."

"Ok, Evan." His mother brushed at her eyes and tried not to look hurt. "I didn't think it would hurt to invite her over. We all have to eat." She turned back to the stove.

Damn. He should have stayed home and ate out of can. The last thing he wanted to do was upset his mother, but he wasn't about to be bribed into marriage by a pot roast, even his mother's pot roast. Faith returned pulling Claire along with her.

"Claire's here," she all but sang.

"Claire, it's good to see you." He nodded to her. "I'll leave you ladies to chat. I need to find Dad," he said curtly and left the room.

"Is something wrong?" Claire asked.

"My brother doesn't like to be teased. Apparently, he can dish it out, but he can't take it," Faith crowed.

"Don't worry about him, dear. Have a seat. Dinner will be ready in a few minutes," Margaret said to Claire then leveled her gaze at her daughter. "There will be no more teasing today. We're all going to have a nice dinner together."

"I'll stop, if he does."

"Faith Ann Bertrand. Don't make me say it again."

"Yes, ma'am," Faith muttered and hung her head.

Giggling from the living room broke the tension. Claire turned to see Hannah peeking around the side of a recliner obviously amused.

"What's so funny, Hannah?" Claire asked.

"Maw Maw fussed at Mom."

"And why is that funny?" Faith snapped.

"Because you're a grownup."

Margaret put her hand on her hip and huffed out a breath. "She may be a grown up, but I'm still her mama. Now, you go find the men and tell them to wash up. I'm about to put the food on the table."

The meal passed pleasantly. Claire noticed that anytime the conversation turned to anything personal Evan tensed up. She asked about the stray and that kept the conversation rolling for a while. She loved the way his face lit up when he told of the lucky dog, Lucky, meeting his new owners. Faith asked about their night out and the change that immediately came over him was noticeable to everyone.

"We had a lovely time. I had never been there. Have you?" she asked his parents. She tried to keep the conversation light and maneuvered it to the band and music in general. Finally Evan began to relax again. She realized at some point that he hadn't expected her to be there. Was this pushing? Not wanting to be rude to her host she planned to finish the meal and then make her excuses to head home. There were always papers to grade and lesson plans to go over.

Once the meal had ended, the cleanup started and Margaret put the coffee on. She tried to leave but there was no way she was leaving before the cake was cut. Hannah made sure to tell her all about the cake she and her mother made just for Claire. She was touched by the sentiment and couldn't remember anyone ever making a cake for her, except her mom.

As she sat there listening to their chatter, and feeling the ease with which they interacted with each other, Claire was reminded again of a dance. These people were family. Their lives were intertwined in a comfortable routine of traditions that would carry from generation to generation. She felt saddened suddenly. Somewhere along the line her family ties had been broken and she was alone.

Evan grabbed her hand under the table. She saw the concern in his face as he asked her if she was ok. She smiled at him. "Yeah, I think so."

This family, his family, had done nothing but try to make her feel at home since she moved here. Was it possible that she could be a part of this? As his hand squeezed hers, she imagined it as the link that would re-connect her to a family. Claire started humming to herself. *Don't stop thinking about tomorrow. Don't stop, it'll soon be here.* Faith cut the cake and placed the first piece on a plate. Hannah brought it to Claire. "I feel like it's my birthday."

"Want us to sing to you?"

"No, that's ok, but promise me that when it is my birthday we can all do this again."

"Yes, we can make another cake. Mom?" Hannah asked Faith hopefully.

"Of course. We'll make it really special."

Later as Evan walked Claire back to her house, he couldn't help but feel that he had acted like a jerk.

"I'm sorry if I made you feel uncomfortable. My sister was being a pain before you got there."

"Oh, I'm sorry."

"For what?"

"For intruding on your family."

"You were invited."

"But not by you. You had no idea I was coming, right?"

"No, but it doesn't matter."

"Yes, I think it does. I think maybe I'm pushing too much."

"What?"

"Nothing, you know where to find me if you need me."

His eyes narrowed on her face searching out a sign of cattiness implied with the statement. It didn't fit with the Claire he knew. If he actually knew her. His suspicion was piqued. His turn of thoughts had him physically stepping back.

"Yeah, that reminds me. I'm going on nights, so I won't be around much for a couple weeks."

"Oh, ok." Claire tried to hide her disappointment. "So I guess I'll see you later then."

"Yeah, later," he repeated then turned and walked away.

Claire stood at her gate wondering what had just happened. She wanted to call him back, but didn't know if that would be considered pushing. Feeling miserable, she latched the gate behind her and went to find Rosie. A good cry in a hot bath then maybe a movie with her overgrown lap dog. It wasn't how she had imagined ending the day, but it was what she knew she could count on.

CHAPTER 15

The days managed to pass even though they seemed drab and gray to Claire. She went to work, smiled and laughed at the children. She visited with Serena and prepared for the Halloween festival. The sun rose and set without any word from Evan. Life went on. She waited for her phone to ring or a knock at her door, over a week had passed and still nothing. She hadn't even caught a glimpse of him next door or in town.

Serena assured her that everything would be ok, but she feared she had messed it up for good. A fatal misstep that had brought an end to the dance. She sighed as she looked through her kitchen window at the fading light.

Her muffled ringtone woke her from her pity party. She looked around frantically for her purse not remembering where she dropped it. The faint sound of music seemed to be coming from a pile of bags, books, and shoes at the front door. It was definitely time to stop feeling sorry for herself and clean up she thought as she snatched up her purse and took out the phone hoping to see Evan's number on the screen. No such luck. It was Debra.

"Hey Mom," Claire sighed into the phone.

"Well, hey there, babe. You're a hard person to track down." Richie's raspy voice seemed to snake through the phone and caress her body.

Claire started to shake, her voice froze in her throat letting out an odd sounding croak. She felt ill when he started to laugh at her.

"What's a matter Claire? Did you actually think I wouldn't find you?"

How had she ever thought his voice was sexy? She couldn't remember anything but the feel of his rough hands on her.

"How did you get Mom's phone?" Claire whispered.

"It wasn't easy. That bitch of a mother you have wasn't being very helpful, so I had to get a little creative."

"M--mom?" she croaked out. Suddenly her legs felt like jelly and the phone like a slippery weight. "Did you hurt her?"

"No, Claire. I didn't hurt her. You jealous?"

"What do you want?"

"You know what I want. I want to see you Claire. I miss you, so tell me where you are?"

"No. I don't want to see you."

"It's not that easy Claire. You don't get to just walk away."

Claire felt like she couldn't breathe. She looked around her messy living room and reached for the door. She needed air. Rosie heard the door open and came rushing past her. Claire stumbled onto the porch and fell to her knees.

"Why?" She gulped at the fresh air as it seemed to

swirl around her, cooling her feverish skin.

"Why? Why what?"

"Why do you want to see me? Why now? You didn't care about me." The cool air seemed to help her find herself.

"I see you've still got that sassy mouth. That's ok, I'll take care of that when I see you."

"No. I don't want to see you, Richie. It's over. I've moved on, you should too."

"You will tell me where you are. If I have to find you on my own it won't be pretty when I do."

"No. It's over."

"Really? Maybe I'll just have to chat with mommy dearest before I leave. Let her know I'm here."

Bile rose up in her throat. "No, leave my mom alone."

"That's up to you, Claire. Tell me where you are and your mom doesn't need to be involved."

Claire sat back in defeat. She was sweating again, the sick rolling around in her stomach.

Not knowing what else to do she whispered, "Cypress Point."

Numbly hanging up the phone, she sat there on the porch staring into the darkness. Nothing's changed. She was foolish to think it could ever be different. She had tried to change things, but somewhere inside she knew this day would come. She would have to pay for sneaking away.

"Claire?" Someone was calling her name. "Claire, Rosie was out." Faith came up to the porch holding on to Rosie's collar. "What's wrong? Are you ok?"

"Yeah, um. Yeah, I'm fine." She looked at Rosie in a daze. "She must have gotten away from me."

Faith put Rosie in the house and came back to sit

next to her friend. "What happened?"

"Nothing."

"Please don't lie to me. I've seen that look before. Sadly, in the mirror."

"Richie just called me. I thought I was safe here."

Faith's eyes widened. "Wow, the cards were right."

"Yeah, I guess so."

"Do you think he's going to cause trouble?"

"Probably. I don't want to see him, but I don't want him bothering my mother."

"I think we need to call Evan." Faith reached for her phone.

"No. Please don't bother him," Claire said into her hands, rubbing them over her face, "I've messed things up enough already."

"What are you talking about?"

"I pushed too soon, the cards were right about that too. He's avoiding me."

"He's working."

"Exactly, and I don't want to bother him with this." Claire stood suddenly and reached for the door. Turning back to Faith, she smiled sadly then added, "Look, I've got to see about Rosie and get my plans ready for school. I'll be fine. Thanks for bringing Rosie back. He just caught me off guard, that's all."

Once Faith convinced herself Claire would be ok, she dialed Evan's number as she walked back across the yard. Evan was clear across the parish on patrol when his phone buzzed. Looking at the screen, he groaned but answered. "Yeah."

"Evan. Where are you?"

"What's wrong?"

"It's Claire."

Panic rose as he pulled off of the highway and parked. "What happened?"

"She's ok. I think."

"You think?"

"Are you avoiding her?"

"What? You called me for that?" Exasperated he pulled the phone away from his ear and gave it a dirty look.

"Look, I just found her sitting on her porch looking pretty bad. Her ex-boyfriend called her."

"And what do you want me to do about it?"

"She was pretty shaken up. I just thought maybe you could check up on her." Faith suggested casually.

"Did she ask you to call me?"

"No. She didn't want me to call you."

"My point exactly. Stop butting in, Faith." Evan snapped.

"Why are you being such a jerk? I thought you cared about her."

"Look, I don't know much about her. Now her boyfriend's back in the picture, so there you go." He gave a shrug to add emphasis even though his sister couldn't see him.

"What if she doesn't want him to be in the picture?"

"That's up to her, ain't it?" he said through clenched teeth.

"I think she's afraid of him," Faith blurted out.

"Why do you say that?"

"He's been bothering her mom trying to find her."

"Faith, I can't stop someone from bothering her."

"No, not bothering her like that weasel Dale Hicks."

"Dale Hicks?" Evan sat up straighter, "What the

hell? Now he's bothering her too?"

"Yeah, but he bothers everybody. I mean like threatening her…"

Evan slammed his free hand on the dashboard. "Dale Hicks threatened Claire? That piece of…"

"NO, Evan. Not Dale Hicks." Faith's voice rose higher with aggravation.

"Who threatened Claire?" Evan asked losing patience.

"The ex-boyfriend, I think."

"Ok, if someone is threatening her she needs to make a report. I'm going to hang up now, Faith. I don't know what kind of game you're playing or she's playing, but I have work to do. I got to go."

He spent the rest of the night fuming and rolling things around in his mind. Was Faith just messing with him? Well, he wouldn't put it past her, but something wasn't sitting right with him. He thought back to the first time he saw Claire clinging to his fence, covered in mud and afraid of him.

Nothing was ever what it seemed.

She came to him the first time they were together. Was she playing him? To what purpose? He didn't know much about her and she hadn't wanted to talk much about herself. He realized now thinking back that she had avoided the subject and turned the conversation away from her past whenever the opportunity arose.

No, nothing was ever what it seemed.

CHAPTER 16

That bitch is going to get what's coming to her, Richie thought as he drove along the interstate looking for the exit that would get him closer to this place called Cypress Point. He had thought she'd go running back to her mother. The last few months he had been following Debra around hoping she'd lead him to Claire. No such luck.

Her friends wouldn't talk to him and the school office would only say she no longer worked there. He had staked out other nearby schools thinking she would have transferred nearby. When that didn't pan out, he started stalking Debra.

He would have never thought Claire had it in her to leave. Just disappear. He had to admit when he came home and found her gone he was glad. He wouldn't have to put up with her bullshit and her constant nagging.

Then it dawned on him. She had taken everything. Just like a woman. In all honesty, she had left everything of his, the TV, stereo, and his gaming chair. She had even left him a few dishes and a pot in the kitchen. Stupid bitch. Still looking out for him. But sweet little Claire didn't realize she had inadvertently taken something that didn't belong to her, or him for that matter. The people it did belong to wanted it back, and they were serious.

His plan hadn't worked out the way he had hoped and now the only way to save his own sorry ass was to find Claire and get it back. They were after him, true, but somewhere in the back of his mind he was still scheming to figure a way out. Not just a way out, but to get away clean. That was the game.

Richie was always scheming, since he was a kid. It had started with his mom. What a pushover. All he would have to do was give her a sweet smile and she'd give in to whatever her baby boy wanted. He was so happy to be an only child, it was definitely easier getting what he wanted. His mother doted on him, he guessed because he was an only child and his real father hadn't wanted either of them, so his mother was always trying to make up for that. She had latched herself on to the first guy who showed interest. His step father made a good living, but loved to drink. All he did was work and drink. Richie didn't remember when it started exactly. It seemed it was always that way. His step father getting his load on would start to find reasons to hate all of the world and everyone in it. So when his mom would use the beer money to buy him something he'd been breaking her head about, like a new video game or the latest name brand shoes, it was a justified beat down. His mother would always take the worst of it, but on occasion it would fall on him. He learned to disappear before his step father got home.

Since his mom was such an easy mark, he needed

more of a challenge. New game, find someone, friend or stranger, it didn't matter and see how much he could get out of them without them knowing. Get away clean. That was the goal.

Out of boredom he began tinkering with locks until he knew how they worked and how to open them. Practicing with the ones in his own home first until he had the operation down smooth. Then he moved on to the neighbor's.

He still remembered the thrill of unlocking the door and letting himself into their home. Walking through their rooms and looking through their private possessions. It had been a feeling of complete power. He was hooked. Not because he needed things. Sure, at first, he took change left lying around or small knick knacks that caught his eye. It wasn't about the taking. It was the power of freedom to go where he wanted.

People thought their things were safe at home while they were off at work or out for a good time. He knew different. Nothing was safe and that empowered him. He became bolder in the game, taking more risks.

He started going into homes when he knew people were there. Locked doors, or not. Women, men, old, young, he didn't care. Sometimes he didn't take anything. He would just go in unnoticed and move things around. Just because he could. He would imagine them scratching their heads at misplaced objects and freaking out. Wondering if they were losing their minds or something supernatural was afoot. Sometimes he even stuck around to watch.

One of the biggest thrills for him was going in at night while people slept in their beds. He would just stand over them watching them breathe. Rich or poor, they were powerless as they lay there dreaming.

The days before home alarms became popular were his best memories. Advancements in home security had definitely limited his freedom to go where he chose. The power of that freedom was important when you came from a place where you had none. Just as the scheming and sneaking grew out of boredom, so did his drug habit.

It wasn't poverty. His family had been considered middle class, even though they weren't rich and couldn't afford certain luxuries they had more than enough to survive by societies standards. So poverty wasn't a reason for getting high. Boredom was. It was just another escape from his doting mother and his inebriated step-father. Another way to say, *Hey, you have no power over me.*

At the same time it offered plenty of opportunities for theft. Money, drugs, whatever. Half the time they didn't remember who was hanging around, if they used it or gave it away.

Which was why he was in the predicament he was in now, driving to some ass backwards town in the middle of the swamp all because he had taken a risk. Well, so be it. That was the game. Sometimes the risk worked out in your favor, sometimes it landed you in deep shit.

His ace in the hole was Claire. They didn't know about Claire. She had timed her exit perfectly. He couldn't argue with that but it pissed him off that she had taken that control away.

He'd punish her for that. Sweet little Claire had a talent for pushing his buttons. He'd be more than happy to show her he was still in control if he got the chance. It just depended on how things played out.

He remembered the first time they had met at a mutual friend's party. She hadn't acted like a school teacher. No teacher he had ever had anyways. She had danced and laughed and flirted with him. He just sat back, watching and waiting. Girls like Claire always went for the silent moody type. It was all a game.

Women. They started out all happiness and laughter till they got you hooked. Then the bitching and nagging started. He knew that game too, and he had played her right back. Richie had let Claire flirt and tease. Then pretended to fall for her. After a few short weeks of acting like the adoring boyfriend, he moved her into his apartment. Slowly but in no uncertain terms he had showed her who was really in control. It had been so easy. She was in love, and that was the biggest scam of all. It was his mother all over again. He'd come home wasted, she'd bitch. He'd say "Sorry, I love you baby" and that was that. Nights when he wasn't feeling so generous he'd skip right to the point, and smack her around a bit to remind her of her place. She'd come round right fast enough, crying and begging. It had sickened him and pleased him at the same time.

Richie finally saw the exit he needed and decided to stop for gas. He could ask around to see how many hours to Cypress Point. Once there, he'd give Claire a call. If he could find her place, he'd be in and out before anyone knew. Working it out in his head and weighing the risk against the desire to show her she still wasn't in control. The people that were after him didn't know about Claire. So in his mind, if he could get the stash and disappear, he'd be back in control. That had been his plan all along, but her mother wouldn't return his calls, so he had lifted her phone and got the number himself.

He laughed out loud as he thought of how close he had come to being caught. He had let himself in their home to search for an address book or some clue to where Claire had run off to. Debra and her new man had come home unexpectedly. He had hidden in the shadows as they went about their evening routine. Seeing Debra's phone in her purse he knew he could at least get her number. He waited until she left the room and slipped the phone out of her purse. He quickly scrolled through her contacts to find Claire's number. He entered it into his phone. Then smiled to himself as he thought how freaked out Claire would be to get a call from him on her mom's phone. So he had slipped outside to make the call. It had the desired effect. He had been so pleased with himself he almost didn't notice Debra had returned to the kitchen. Thankfully she had her back to him as she searched through the pantry. Here she was in her tastefully decorated kitchen with her new husband and she thought she was safe. He could have easily reached out and touched her. It had been tempting. Instead, he placed her phone with Claire's number still on the display screen in the middle of the counter. He smiled to himself as he melted back into the shadows and let himself quietly out the back door.

Richie pulled into a gas station to fill up and grab a drink. He looked around for an easy mark as he entered the store. Maybe he should have picked a busier station he thought to himself, fishing a drink from the cooler. He was almost out of money and sick of sleeping in his car. He had been snatching a few bucks here and there without calling too much attention to himself. The further he got from the city the harder it became. Being a stranger in these small towns was like having a flashing arrow sign over your head.

Richie flashed his best smile at a pretty young mother who had pulled up to the adjacent pump. She blushed and looked away as she grabbed for the toddlers hand before he could run off. Richie followed her with his eyes as she went inside the store apparently to take the kid to the restroom. He paced a bit and made a show of stretching as he peeked into the car. Whoop, there it was amid the sippy cup and cookie wrappers, sat an open purse with a bank envelope peeping out. It was screaming *Take Me, Take Me Now!* Richie smiled as he quickly reached in through the open window and snagged the money right out of the envelope. He didn't even bother with the wallet. Cash was always better. He stuffed the money in his pocket as he thought of his reunion with Claire.

Back on the road, a highway this time, he looked around at the miles of farmland before him. He hated being out of the city. He felt like he was a mark out in the open with no where to hide. In the city, there were so many nooks and crannies and crowds. He loved the crowds. He could disappear into a crowd easily with his ordinary looks. He kept his blond hair trimmed. Not too long, not too short, nothing weird or memorable. His face was an ordinary face. The boy next door. No one ever looked twice at him. The few times he had ventured out of the city thinking country people would be easier targets, he realized it was harder to hide in the wide open spaces and the people were very leery of strangers. If he needed more money, which he knew he would if he couldn't get to Claire's today, he'd have to be very careful how he got it.

A few more turns from this high way to that one, and suddenly he was out of road. The lousy Louisiana highway had dead ended in the middle of some kind of field. He had no clue what was growing in it and he didn't care. *"Shit! Shit! Shit!"* he muttered to himself as he backed up and turned the car around. He would have to backtrack until he found where he made the wrong turn. An hour later, he found himself on the right highway headed in the right direction.

Another hour passed as he noticed the farmland had gradually turned into trees. Except these trees seemed to be growing out of the water. Richie cursed Claire again. What had she been thinking coming way out here? He wondered if she'd purposely picked this place because she knew he'd never look for her here. If it wasn't a matter of life or death, namely his life or death, he wouldn't even be looking for her. He wouldn't be caught dead in this God forsaken place. He laughed at himself as the irony of his thought struck him. He certainly hoped he wouldn't be caught dead or alive in this God forsaken place.

Finally, a green road sign up ahead declared his journey was over. He had reached his destination: Cypress Point. He looked over the small town decorated to the max for Halloween. Storefronts and homes sported smiling jack o' lanterns and skeletons. The traditional orange and black seemed to be draped everywhere. *Only in a small town*, he thought as he shook his head.

A glance at his watch told him that his wrong turn had put him way behind, but Claire should be at school for at least another hour. So if he found where she was staying quickly, he could be in and out fast. He thought it over. He hated drawing attention to himself if it wasn't required. He knew he'd stick out in this small town especially if he started asking questions about Claire. Pulling out his phone he decided the best course of action was to just ask her right out. If she wasn't cooperative, he could wait at the school and hope she didn't make a scene.

Send me your address. be there today or tomorrow. He texted to her.

He was pleased with himself as he pulled into the diner. She wouldn't be expecting him so soon, if everything went smoothly no one would ever know he'd been here. He retrieved the stolen money from his pocket hoping it would be enough for a good steak. *Jackpot!* Richie thought as he counted out the twenty's and slid into a booth. Eighty dollars was enough for a steak dinner and gas to get out of town. A waitress came to take his order and asked if he was in town for the festival.

"No, just passing through."

As his eyes wandered from side to side taking in the surroundings he plotted what he'd do first when this shit town was in his rear view mirror.

Claire's message came as his food arrived. Just the address, nothing extra like "Can't wait to see you", or "I've missed you." He smirked as he cut into his rare steak. Maybe she had moved on. Her love had been a misplaced and totally useless emotion anyway. Well, maybe not totally useless. It had kept his bills paid for a few years. His phone buzzed again.

Won't be home today. Festival. Tomorrow is better.

He thought it over as he ate. Was she just stalling? Had she found his hiding place? Only one way to find out. If he couldn't get inside her place today, he knew he'd have time tomorrow. As he glanced out the window a flyer caught his attention. Cypress Point Halloween Festival. She wasn't lying about that so maybe she hadn't found it. Mulling it over as he called for the check, he decided this festival might actually be a good thing. As the waitress cleared his table he asked, "Where can I get a Halloween mask?"

"A few doors down at the dollar store. You decided to stay for the festival?" She smiled down at him.

"I'm thinking about it. Sounds like fun."

He texted Claire back one letter. **k**. Let her think she was in control and safe for now. Richie knew better. He whistled as he walked down to the store. A mask might come in handy.

Finding her house had been easy. When he saw the picket fence he snorted. So like Claire. She wanted her life to be some kind of fairy tale. He watched from across the street for a while before getting out of the car. Most of the houses seemed to be empty, except for the one next door. An elderly couple was moving around in the back yard. Going in the back door wouldn't be an option. Chances were they'd notice him. He hated risking the front door. You never knew when someone would drive by. It would be getting dark soon, but everyone would be getting home. He looked down the street again and figured now was as good a time as any.

Walking up to the front of the house he made sure the old people wouldn't notice him. The door, like the house, was older. He was sure the lock would be no problem. Walking onto the porch, he glanced through the front window. Seeing the familiar old lumpy flowered sofa, he was certain he had the right place.

His experienced, confident hands knew their work. His left hand gently worked the pick, caressing the worn old tumblers, while his right hand pantomimed knocking on the door. To anyone watching from behind he appeared to be waiting for someone to answer the door.

When the pick lined the tumblers up, he ran the wrench in and the knob turned freely in his hand. He heard a vehicle approaching as he opened the door. Quickly closing the door behind him he peeked through the window to get a look at the car. Great, a cop showing up at the neighbor's. What were the odds? He scanned the living room looking for what was his. A noise in the back of the house alerted him that someone was there. Shit. Did Claire have someone living with her? He hadn't even considered that.

A whimper followed by a snort. A dog? Richie tensed. In one motion he pocketed his tools, leaning forward on the balls of his feet, bracing himself in case the animal came right at him. The trained ones always did. No growl. No bark. Just sudden.

The padding of what sounded like large feet coming down the hallway had Richie moving towards the door. A huge black and white dog stopped at the end of the hallway looking confused. It snorted again, then let out a series of ear ringing woofs.

Richie felt for the door knob behind him, and let himself out. Once the door was between him and the beast, he let out a sigh of relief. His relief was not long lived. The cop was walking up to the porch. He plastered a smile on his face.

"Can I help you officer?"

"Deputy. Maybe. Is Claire home?"

"Ah, no. She's still at school. Won't be home till later."

"And you are?"

"An old friend of Claire's, just here for a visit."

"The old boyfriend?" the deputy asked as he narrowed his dark eyes at Richie.

Unable to stop himself, Richie's jaw clenched in a sudden jolt of anger. So the bitch had been telling people about him. Forcing a smile, he shrugged it off. "Yeah, that would be me. Trying to decide if we can work it out, you know?"

"Hmm. Well, good luck to you. Sounds like Rosie wants out," he said nodding his head towards the house and the muffled barking coming from within.

"Oh, yeah. I'm not sure Rosie likes me. Maybe I should wait for Claire to let her out."

"Maybe so," he answered as he turned to walk away.

"You live next door?"

"No, my parents do. Enjoy your visit," the deputy called over his shoulder as he walked towards the house next door.

Damn it, this trip is not turning out as I planned, Richie thought to himself.

Once the cop was out of sight, he made his way back to his car. He'd have to figure out a way around the dog. Damn, he hated dogs. He'd try again tonight. Everyone would be at the festival. He would try again or be waiting for her when she got home.

CHAPTER 17

Evan watched from his parents' kitchen window as Claire's boyfriend drove away. He didn't like him and if Rosie didn't like him either, something was wrong with him.

"Oh, Evan. I wasn't expecting you," his mother said from behind him.

"Hey, Mom. Just thought I'd stop by before work."

"What are you looking at?"

"Nothing."

"Is it Claire? Why don't you just go talk to her?" she asked pushing past Evan to open a cabinet.

"No, it's not Claire. She's not home. How long has her boyfriend been there?"

"Her boyfriend? She doesn't have a boyfriend." Margaret said pulling a pot out of the cabinet.

"Her old boyfriend. How long has he been staying with her?"

"Nobody's staying with her." Margaret turned giving Evan her full attention, "What old boyfriend?"

"Mom, I just talked to him. He was coming out of her house."

"Evan, I don't know what you're talking about."

"Where's Faith? She called me about him yesterday."

"What? Claire's never mentioned a boyfriend and Faith didn't say anything about it to me."

"Where's Faith?"

"She left to pick up the kids. She should be back soon.... I'm sure they are all getting ready for the Festival," Margaret said obviously flustered. "He was in her house?" she asked peering out the window.

"He's gone now, Mom. Just keep an eye out. Something's not right with that guy. I don't like him."

"Well, of course you don't like him. You just need to go talk to Claire. I'm sure it's just a misunderstanding."

"Whatever. Like I told Faith, not my business."

"Then why did you go over there?"

"Because I saw a strange man coming out of her house." His mother looked at him knowingly. "What?"

"Whatever you say dear. I'm sure everything's going to be fine." Smiling she put the pot on the stove. "Are you hungry?"

"No, I gotta get to work. Tell Faith...never mind. I'll call her myself." He punched in her number as he walked back to his SUV.

"Hey," Faith answered on the first ring.

"Hey. Where are you?"

"Bringing the kids to town to get some things for their costumes. Why? Is something wrong?"

"No," he said then sighed, "I don't know."

"What do you mean?"

"Well, I ran into Claire's boyfriend today, according to him they're trying to work things out. So maybe you should just stay out of it and leave me out of it, too."

"What? You saw Richie?"

"Richie?" Evan gave a snort, "Is that his name?"

"Yeah, you talked to him?"

"That's what I'm trying to tell you. He seemed to think they were trying to get back together."

"No. Claire doesn't want to have anything to do with him. I told you she didn't want to see him."

"I find that hard to believe. Stop playing games."

"Why don't you believe me?"

"He was coming out of her house, Faith. If she didn't want to see him, I don't think she'd let him in her house while she was at work."

"Her house? Oh my God. Is he there now?"

"No. He left. I'm assuming he'll go back." Evan glanced over at Claire's house again. "He seemed to be making himself at home."

"No, no. Evan. Something's not right. She didn't want to see him and the cards were warning her about it."

"What the hell are you talking about?" Yanking open his door, he stopped and looked back at the house.

"Serena. The card reading. I overheard them talking about it."

"Oh geesh. Have you completely lost your mind?" He slid behind the wheel and slammed his door.

"No I'm serious."

"Look, if she's letting him stay with her there's nothing I can do about it. If she doesn't want him there, she needs to tell him to leave. If he doesn't, then she needs to call the station."

"I'm gonna call her. She would have said

something, I know it."

"Sis, maybe you should try minding your own business."

"Good-bye Evan."

"Later."

Claire was just parking her car in her driveway when her phone started playing her theme song. She turned off the ignition and answered as she tried to gather up her books. "Hello?"

"Where are you?"

"Oh, hey Faith. I'm just getting home."

"Look, I know it's none of my business, but is Richie staying at your house?"

"What? No. Why?"

"Evan just called me."

"Ok." Slamming her door closed with her hip she turned toward her house.

"He talked to Richie today and he was at your house."

"What?" Claire froze in her tracks and the books started to slide out of her grip. "He was here?"

"Look, stay outside till I get there."

"What? No. I need to check on Rosie."

"I'll be there in a few minutes."

"Ok, I gotta go."

She ran for the door. She called for Rosie as she grabbed the knob and fumbled with the keys. The door was unlocked. Claire stood there staring at the knob with her heart pounding. She opened it slowly. Rosie was there in an instant obviously happy to see her. She hugged her tight not caring that Rosie was drooling all over her.

"Ok, girl. Let's get you out in the back yard."

After putting Rosie out, she went room by room looking for any clue that someone had been in her house.

Faith came in the front door holding all of her books. "I picked these up for you. Is everything ok?"

"Yeah, thanks. Come in and sit down." Grabbing the books from Faith she sat on the sofa, "Tell me again what Evan said."

"Well, he told me to mind my own business. Like that's gonna happen." Faith snorted as she sat next to Claire.

"But he said Richie was here?"

"Yes, he said he was coming out of your house and he told Evan y'all were trying to work things out."

"No, I haven't even seen him. He said he was coming by tomorrow, but that's over."

"Is anything missing?" Faith glanced around nervously.

"No, not that I can tell."

Claire shivered as she thought of Richie walking through her house and touching her things. Thank God Rosie was ok. She didn't think he'd hurt her but Richie was hard to read and easily angered.

"How did he get in?"

"I don't know, but my front door was unlocked when I got home."

"Claire, I don't like this. If he comes back here, you need to call someone." Faith hesitated for a moment then sighed. "The kids are waiting to get their costumes on. I need to get them ready. Are you gonna be ok?"

"Yes. I have got to get going too. I just came home to see about Rosie and grab my costume.

Serena's there already. I have been looking forward to this since I moved here. I hope Richie doesn't spoil it."

"We won't let him. We're right next door. You run over to my parents' if you need to."

Claire teared up at that statement. She knew these people wouldn't let anything happen to her if they could help it. This family that had taken her in and made her feel like a part of theirs. There was a strength in knowing you weren't alone. She knew without a doubt that if she needed Evan he would be there, too. No matter how he was acting now.

She would have loved to see the conversation between those two. A thought occurred to her. Evan was at her house, too. Had he come to see her? She smiled to herself as she gathered up her costume and fortune cookies. This year for Halloween maybe she'd get a treat. A tall, dark treat named Evan.

CHAPTER 18

The school children anxiously awaited the last bell of the day. Their thoughts focused on running home to put on costumes to wait for sunset. The town itself had been adorned in Halloween finery and tonight was the magical night. From the park down main street to the school parking lot people were setting up tables and booths. The costume contest was set for 4:30pm and by the time the awards were handed out, the bright October sun would give way to a cool crisp night. The weather forecast had called for a chance of showers after midnight due to a cold front pushing through the area. Louisiana weather was so unpredictable, but the festivities should be well over by then.

Claire's excitement was dampened by a feeling of dread. Just knowing Richie was here somewhere had her nervously looking over her shoulder.

"Are you going to be ok?" asked Serena from behind a curtain she was trying to hang.

"Yes," Claire said reaching up to help pull the length of curtain over the make shift frame. "I just wish he would have waited until tomorrow. I don't want him causing a scene."

"He was in your house, Claire."

"I don't know how."

"What I don't understand is why he just didn't wait for you there?"

"I don't know. He was never fond of dogs. Maybe Rosie scared him off, or Evan. Who knows?" Claire smoothed the curtain out and stepped back. "What do you think?"

"It looks great!" Serena covered the table with a velvet cloth. "Let's read your cards again while we have time."

"No, the costume contest should be starting soon."

"I'm still having that dream. I don't like this."

"I'll be fine," Claire said with more confidence than she felt.

She didn't want to be scared of Richie but in all honesty, she was. She had no idea of what he wanted or why he was even here, but she knew it wasn't going to be a happy reunion. She didn't need the cards to tell her that.

Deciding that Richie wouldn't ruin this night for her, she looked at her friend and all the work they had done.

"I brought my camera. Let's find someone to take pictures of us. We look good."

Coming out of the tent, she spotted Dale Hicks dressed in pirate garb heading straight for them. Serena snorted behind her. "Here we go. Get the napkins ready, and be prepared to be drooled on."

"Wow! You girls look great!" Dale called out as he approached eyeing the tent. "So, can I play too?"

"In your dreams," Serena muttered under her breath.

"Hey Dale. Do me a favor and take a few pictures of us."

"Sure," he said eagerly reaching for the camera. "Should we go inside?"

"I guess we can take some inside too," Claire said and looked over at Serena who rolled her eyes and sighed.

Dale seemed to be enjoying giving them posing directions a little too much. All of which gave him an excuse to touch them. Move your arm over. Turn your head this way. Move in a little closer together. His obvious enjoyment was making Claire uncomfortable and judging by Serena's growls she was growing impatient.

"Ok, let's go back outside and take a few in front of the tent," Claire suggested.

"Oh...ok," Dale said with obvious disappointment as he followed them out of the tent. Claire and Serena stood in front of the tent as he positioned himself to take the picture. After a few snaps of the camera he stopped and reached out to pull Claire's blouse further down off of her shoulder.

"Stop it, Dale." Claire pushed his hand away and readjusted her blouse.

"Oh, come on. Show a little bit of skin. It'll make a better picture." He gave her a suggestive grin.

"The picture isn't for you, freak. Take it and be gone," Serena hissed at him. Not bothered by Serena's insult he tugged on Claire's blouse again.

"Yeah, but I want a copy." He winked at her.

"Hicks, she said to stop it." The sound of Evan's rough voice made them all jump.

"Evan." Claire barely recognized her own voice. It seemed to come from somewhere else.

"Oh, hey. It's Deputy Dog. Good, you can take a picture of the three of us together," Dale said snidely.

"I don't think so," Evan said as he grabbed the camera from Dale and stood directly in front of Claire and Serena. "I think you've worn out your welcome. Move on."

"I didn't get my reading yet," Dale protested.

"We're not open yet. Come back after the costume contest," Serena snapped.

Claire was still frozen in place. She couldn't take her eyes off of Evan. She had only caught glimpses of him in uniform, mostly in his car. Wowser. She knew he looked good in his jeans. Correction, he looked damn good in his jeans, but this kicked the sexiness level up several notches as far as she was concerned. It must be the Alpha male thing. She knew her mouth was open, but she was having a hard time closing it.

Evan watched as Dale walked away then turned to Claire and Serena, his dark eyes glittering dangerously.

"Evan saves the day again. You, sir, are my hero." Serena curtsied.

"I heard he's been bothering you."

"He is a pesky little freak. He makes a habit of hanging around the gym when we have belly dancing class."

Evan looked down at the camera in his hand then back at Claire. "Do you still want a picture?"

"Um, no. I think we got some good ones," Claire answered still struggling to find her voice.

"Here, how about I take one of you guys?" Serena grabbed the camera from Evan and pushed him at Claire. His arms went around her automatically pulling her to him. As Claire looked up into his dark eyes she heard the camera snap.

"Ok, now look at me and smile," Serena directed as she snapped a few more pictures.

"I need to talk to you," Evan said into her ear sending a shiver down her spine. She nodded in agreement and pulled him into the tent.

"Don't play games with me, Claire," he said before she could even open her mouth.

"Games?"

"What are you playing at?" he asked gruffly.

"I don't know what you're talking about."

"Richie. He told me y'all were trying to work things out."

"No. That's not true. We are not getting back together. I don't even know why he's here."

"Then why was he at your house? Why was he in your house?"

"I don't know. He said he wasn't coming until tomorrow. I don't know how he got in."

Evan's eyes narrowed on her. "Are you telling me he broke into your house?"

"I guess so. I know I locked the door, but the back door, if it wasn't shut...." Not knowing what else to say she shrugged.

"Did you report it?"

"No. Nothing was missing."

Evan rubbed his hands over his face and sighed. "Claire, if he was in your house without your permission you should at least report it .... unless, there's some reason why you don't want to."

"I just don't see the point." She looked down at the ground.

"You're making excuses for him, so you must like

the attention."

Her head snapped back up. "What?"

"Just like with Hicks. You like the attention."

"No, I don't. How can you think that?"

"You didn't say anything," he said simply.

"I told him to stop it."

"You let him pull on your shirt and you didn't do anything. Just like you let some guy in your house without reporting him."

"That's not fair." Claire could feel her cheeks burning with that old familiar shame. "I wouldn't have even known he was in my house if you hadn't seen him. I haven't seen or heard from him in almost a year. I don't *want* to see him. I moved here to get away from him."

"Then why did you agree to see him."

"I didn't agree."

"You're not making any sense. If we're gonna keep seeing each other I need to know what's going on."

Claire sucked in a breath. "You want us to keep dating? Like we're a couple?" Her blue eyes shone with hope.

"Damn it, woman. Talk to me. Did you invite him here or not?" He grabbed her by the shoulders.

"No," she said firmly then added softly, "but I did give him my address."

Evan dropped his hands in defeat. Tears burned Claire's eyes.

"If you didn't want to see him then why would you give him the address?"

"Because I was afraid he'd hurt my mom," she whispered trying desperately to hold back the tears.

"He threatened your mom?" Evan asked incredulously. "And you didn't say anything?"

"Everything ok in there?" Serena called from outside the tent. "We've got customers lining up out here."

"Look, I can't explain everything right now. I don't know why he's here. I just need you to know there's no one else but you. I promise."

She ran from the tent with tears streaming down her face. Evan sat in a chair, dumbfounded. What in the hell was going on? He had felt something wasn't right, but this wasn't what he was expecting. Serena poked her head in the tent.

"Everything ok?"

"I don't know. You tell me. You're the fortune teller."

She smiled as she entered the tent and sat across the table from him. "I can read your cards, if you want. You can be the first customer."

"No, I want you to tell me what's going on with Claire. Who's this Richie guy?"

"Look, Evan, I'm worried too. From what she's told me this guy is bad news. I'm really afraid for her."

"He's hurt her before?"

"Yes, he's sent her to the ER a couple of times."

"Damn it." He slammed his fist on the table. "Why didn't she say something?"

"She was embarrassed. She moved away to start over. Now he's here."

"I have to work tonight or I would have her come home with me."

"I've already asked her to come stay at my house tonight. He won't find her there and she can stay as long as she needs to."

"Alright. I'm going to be keeping an eye out for

him. If she sees him, I want to know about it."

"Of course."

"I've got to get back out there." He stood up and turned to exit the tent.

"Evan," Serena called as he opened the curtain. He turned back with worry heavy on his brow. "I don't need cards to see you two belong together."

"Yeah, I think you're right. It seems like everyone else could see it, too. It just took me awhile to figure it out for myself."

Evan walked out into the rapidly fading light. The crowd was growing. Groups of children and adults were making their way up the street. Evan followed them as he kept an eye out for Richie. He noticed Richie's car a few blocks down parked on a side street.

Evan glanced around as he approached the vehicle. It was empty except for trash on the floor boards and a pile of clothes on the back seat. From the looks of it Richie had been living in his car. Maybe it was the reason for his sudden reappearance in Claire's life, he needed a paycheck.

Walking around the back of the car, he took note of the Texas plates and decided he should have Richie checked out. Calling in the plate number, he leaned against the car and waited.

Hershey's raspy voice crackled over his radio in answer, "What's wrong Bertrand? Somebody left a dog in the car unattended?"

"Just run it, Squirts." Evan snapped as he let his gaze wander over the growing crowd of festival goers.

"Richard Denton. Houston address. No priors...not even dog napping." Hershey added with a chuckle.

"No record of domestic abuse?" Evan shook his head in frustration. Claire had obviously never filed charges.

"Nah, what did he do? Kick a dog while he was down?"

"Knock it off, asshole."

"Come on, man. Lighten up, I'm just busting your balls."

"Do your job. He was seen coming out of a residence he did not have permission to be in. He also has a rough history with my parent's neighbor. Car is here at the festival. I don't want him causing any trouble."

"Whatever you say, dawg."

Evan bit back a curse as he scanned the crowds for any sign of Richie. Wondering if he'd take the chance to confront Claire here in public. No. He had obviously been careful. Being the kind of coward who got his kicks by threatening women, chances were he'd wait until he had her alone with no witnesses. Evan wasn't planning to give him the chance.

CHAPTER 19

From his vantage point a few booths down, Richie had watched with interest as the deputy approached Claire and the drama that followed. Richie had almost laughed out loud when the deputy grabbed the camera out of the pirate's hand. Then when Claire exited the tent in tears, he snorted behind his mask. Same ol' Claire running away. So the lawdog had a thing for her, that was good to know. He had been startled to see the deputy, almost afraid he'd recognize him. Then he remembered the mask, and thankfully he had thought to add a cheap black cape over his clothes. The crowd was growing by the minute and Richie was feeling more comfortable about being able to walk around without much notice. He planned to keep an eye on Claire. Then when he thought most of the town had shown up he would head back to her house. He wasn't sure what to do about the dog, but he'd figure out something. He wasn't leaving empty handed. He couldn't afford to.

When he felt the festival was in full swing, he made his way back to his car only to find the deputy leaning against it. Damn, he must have noticed the Texas plates. He'd have to go on foot. This was not working out at all like he planned. He lost himself in the crowd, moving in the direction of Claire's house. As he paused to get his bearings and figure out the quickest route to Claire's, he caught a glimpse of the pirate guy that had been bothering Claire and her friend earlier. He was pouring on the charm to another uninterested lady and was turned down flat. *What a loser!* He was trying too hard.

Captain Jack shrugged off the rejection and walked away in search of a more willing companion. The path he was on took him deeper into the park that was thick with giant oak trees dripping with moss. Richie decided to follow him. This guy needed to be taught a lesson and Richie was in the mood to give it to him. Besides, he might need a distraction later to get back to his car. He skirted the path in the shadows, dogging the pirate's every step. The fool was blissfully unaware of Richie's presence.

There it was. Familiar as his face in a mirror and welcoming as a lover in his arms.

Power.

Control.

His senses heightened. A warm rush washed over him, from neck to groin. The stalk became real and his body responded. Richie breathed in deep. He was in control. It was up to him what happened to the jerk in the pirate suit.

The crowd was gone, leaving just the two of them. Captain Jack looked around finally noticing his isolation and the darkness that closed in around him. He had been so intent on searching out new prey, he didn't realize he was now being stalked. The hunter becomes the hunted. Richie grinned behind his mask and purposely rustled the leaves under his feet.

"Who's there?" the pirate called out into the darkness. Richie picked up a rock and threw it behind the pirate causing him to turn around.

"You kids better stop it. I'm in no mood for your pranks tonight," he said with more bravado than he was obviously feeling. Richie could feel his emerging fear.

Richie rushed at him then, grabbing him in a bear hug and pushing him off the path further into the darkness. They fell on the ground in a heap, Richie driving all his weight down on top of his prey. Captain Jack crunched under him pitifully, gasping for breath. Richie didn't give him time to recover. Pummeling his victim with fists that didn't stop until they were moist with blood. The iron smell of it filled his nostrils and he breathed in power. The red faded a bit from his vision as he regarded the now unmoving pirate. Richie searched through his pockets for his keys and wallet. He would hold onto them for now. Just in case he needed a getaway vehicle or a place to hide out. With that deputy hanging around things weren't going as he planned. Always have a way out.

He dragged Captain Jack behind one of the giant oaks. He didn't want anyone finding him too soon. Wiping his bloody hands on his black cape, he started walking in the direction of Claire's house. Once was out of range of the festival noise, he stayed in the shadows making his way through the quiet streets. It looked like most people were downtown. Too bad he was in a hurry. He could have had some fun.

The wind picked up making the tree branches

creak and groan. Wind chimes from a nearby house tinkled wildly and he thought he heard the distant rumble of thunder. A well timed thunderstorm could help his getaway, but if it came too soon everyone would start to head home to beat the rain. Now that he knew the deputy was screwing Claire, he needed to get out before she came home with him in tow. When he came to her street, he decided to cut through the back yards to avoid detection.

Richie jumped the fence into her yard approaching the back door quietly. Remembering the giant dog inside, he paused thinking of his earlier encounter. It hadn't seemed to be very aggressive, but it had barked. Then he remembered the deputy had suggested he let the dog out. *Good advice, Mr. Officer, sir.* He pulled the door knob and to his surprise the door moved. The old wooden door had expanded with the humid weather. It was a bit sticky but opened with a forceful shove. Maybe things were looking up. He called softly to the dog.

"Here doggy, doggy." The giant dog suddenly appeared in the doorway confused by the visitor. Richie held the door open and called again.

"Want to go out, doggy?"

That did the trick. The gangly dog romped past him out into the yard. Richie closed the door behind him and set out looking for the table. He hadn't seen it in the living room earlier, but that didn't mean it wasn't there. Claire was constantly changing furniture around. Some bullshit she probably got out of a magazine. A quick glance around the kitchen then he moved down the hallway to the bedrooms. Searching one then the other, still no sign of the table. His anger grew as he looked in the bathroom.

It wasn't there.

"Fuck. Fuck. Fuck. The dizzy bitch got rid of it!" Richie ranted as he looked around wildly.

It had to be here. If it wasn't there, he could never go back for sure. They'd be waiting for him. Did she sell it? Throw it? His stomach felt sick.

His reflection gazed back at him from the medicine cabinet mirror, "Why get rid of it? She loved that thing."

His eyes narrowed as another thought occurred to him. "Or did she find it and use the money?"

His blood started to boil and rage took over. He smashed the mirror, sending bits of glass flying. Cursing, he swept the bottles and knickknacks off the shelves then ripped the shower curtain from the rod.

He wasn't leaving empty handed. He'd wait for Claire and she'd tell him what she did with his money. One way or another she would tell.

He'd make her tell.

CHAPTER 20

The steady stream of goblins, witches, superheroes and princesses seemed to be never ending. Claire loved every minute of it, from handing out candy and fortune cookies to snapping pictures of the kids in costumes. There were moments when time seemed to stand still and she could almost forget about Richie and the past. Evan had stopped by several times to check on her and she knew he was keeping an eye out for Richie. His car was parked down the street, so he was here somewhere. Claire wanted nothing more than to make a new start with Evan and never look back again.

Judging by the line waiting for card readings over the last few hours, Claire knew her guess about the popularity of the booth was correct. She wished she could give Serena a break, but it was still Greek to her even after the crash course. The line was finally dwindling down. She thought it odd that Dale had never returned for his reading but in all honesty, she was relieved. He was a hopeless flirt and she hated to be rude. She would have to make it very clear that she was unavailable and his advances were unwelcome. She was determined to not let anything come between her and Evan. Including Richie. Knowing she had people that cared for her, she was prepared to stand up to him once and for all. He couldn't seriously believe that they would just pick up where they left off. It was over. He held no power over her anymore. Whatever feelings she had for him were long dead and buried. The only thing she felt when she thought of him was sick.

"Trick or Treat!" Hannah and Trent called out in unison as they approached with treat bags open.

"Look at you two. Pirates and Princesses were definitely popular this year."

"Next year I want to be a zombie. Mom wouldn't let me this year," Trent said with obvious disappointment.

"Oh please. Next year, I promise. This year was just too crazy. I wasn't up for makeup and fake blood." Faith looked tired. Her smile was wistful as she regarded her children.

"You ok?" Claire asked concerned about her friend.

"Yeah. How about you? I just saw Evan. He's looking for Richie. He's here somewhere. His car hasn't moved."

"He told me. If he's here, I haven't seen him." A gust of wind whipped at the tent. Claire grabbed at the curtain to hold it down.

"Wow. Where did that come from?" Faith asked looking at the dark sky.

"We might have storms, but it wasn't supposed to be until after midnight."

"We've made the rounds, so maybe we should

head on home before the rain starts."

"No, Mom, not yet. You said we could get a funnel cake," Hannah protested.

"And go back through the haunted house!" Trent added.

"I don't want to get caught in the rain."

"What's this about a haunted house?" Serena asked as she exited the tent.

"It was great. They had zombies and body parts everywhere. It was great!" Trent said excitedly.

"Apparently, it was great." Faith rolled her eyes and Serena laughed.

"Rave reviews from the zombie fan," Claire agreed as she put candy in their bags.

"I didn't like it. It was gross," Hannah pouted.

"Cause you're a baby," Trent taunted his sister and gave her a shove.

"Am not. Mom!" Hannah shoved back.

"Hey, I tell you what. One night, when it's ok with your mom, you guys can come sleep over at my house. It's a real haunted house," Serena suggested hoping to derail the argument.

"What?" Faith asked wide eyed.

"Yes!!" Hannah jumped up and down.

"Tonight?" Trent asked hopefully.

"No, not tonight. Claire is staying tonight."

"Really? You're sleeping in a haunted house?" Hannah's big eyes shone with awe.

"Yes, but I don't think it's really haunted," Claire assured her.

"You won't go, you're a baby!" Trent teased.

"Yes, I will. I just didn't like the gross stuff. Her house doesn't have gross stuff," Hannah snapped at her brother then turned to Serena. "Does it?"

"No, I don't like gross stuff either, but sometimes spooky stuff does happen. It's really great." Serena smiled at Trent then turned to Claire. "The wind is really kicking. Maybe we should start packing up."

"Yeah, I think it's starting to wind down anyway. I'll help you get everything loaded into your car."

"That's our cue to leave. Say goodnight, kids."

"Awe. Mom."

"Ok, one more time through the haunted house. Then it's home we go." Faith watched as the kids wandered off then turned back to Claire. "You're staying at Serena's?"

"Yes, I'm going to run home and get Rosie. She'll be getting nervous with that storm coming."

"That makes me feel better. I'll let Mom and Dad know too. They've been worried sick since Evan saw Richie coming out of your house."

Claire almost teared up. It was a wondrous feeling having friends and family to care about you. In her years with Richie, she had distanced herself from people because she didn't want them to know. She had been so ashamed, she had isolated herself from everyone including her mom.

"It was either her staying with me or Evan was going to take her on patrol with him," Serena teased.

"He'd do it, too. Brother dear, has finally come around. We will be shopping for wedding dresses before too long. I knew it." Faith smiled knowingly.

"I think if we make it through this night, we've got a good chance," Serena said mysteriously then pointed at Faith. "And then you're next."

"Oh no." Her smile disappeared and she looked at the ground.

"Oh, yes. Remember my dream and even the cards

hinted at a love interest."

"I've got to go. Let's go kids. The haunted house is waiting." Faith rushed off without looking back.

"Well, that was not as much fun as I thought it would be," Serena commented and gave Claire a puzzled look. "What do you think that is about?"

"I don't know. Maybe she just doesn't want to talk about it in front of the kids."

"Hmm. Maybe, but they weren't even listening. They were heading to the funnel cakes." Another gust of wind pulled at the tent almost lifting it off of the ground.

"Let's get this down before the wind takes it."

They hurried to dismantle the tent as the wind continued to increase. Claire was struggling on her tiptoes to get the poles disconnected when a pair of strong hands reached around her to help.

"Oh," she gasped, "I didn't hear you." She smiled up at Evan.

"I think you're a little too short to reach. Let me help before y'all get caught in the rain."

She folded up the curtains and packed them neatly to be carried to Serena's car. Within a few trips under Evan's watchful eye they had everything loaded up.

"You're going home with her, right?"

"I have my car and I need to go pick up Rosie first, but then I promise I will go straight to Serena's and stay put."

"Hey, if you want to jump in, I'll give you a ride to your car," Serena suggested.

"That's ok. I'll walk her," Evan answered. His dark eyes scanning the thinning crowd.

Serena sighed and asked Evan sweetly, "Mmmm, do you have a brother? Cousin?"

Claire laughed at her friend. "Stop it."

"Ok, I'll be waiting for you Claire."

"Thanks Serena. I shouldn't be too far behind you. I just have to get Rosie." Claire waved as her friend drove off.

"I'm parked down here." She motioned awkwardly, suddenly feeling shy. Evan grabbed her hand as they walked and the awkwardness disappeared.

"His car is still parked in the same place."

"I don't know where he could be. I certainly didn't see him."

"I didn't either, but the crowd was pretty big and a lot of people were in costume."

"He could have found me if he wanted to. I wasn't hiding."

"That's what has me worried."

"What do you mean?"

"If he just wanted to confront you, he had plenty of chances to do it. He's been sneaking around and I don't like it. Maybe I should at least follow you back to your house."

"No, there's still people out here, and like you said his car hasn't moved. He's here somewhere. I have your number if I need it."

They stopped walking as they reached her car. Evan looked in it, then scanned the area again. People were making their way back to their cars and others were busy fighting the wind to pack up their booths.

"All right, but if you get home and the door is open. Don't go inside. Go to my parents' and call me from there. Promise me."

"Ok, I will." She leaned up on her tip toes and gave him a quick kiss.

His arms went around her, immediately pulling her closer. "And I will promise you that I won't let him hurt you ever again."

She looked into his dark eyes and saw the honesty and truth. She knew he'd do whatever he could to protect her. He was a man who did not make promises lightly. That warm feeling was back. Trying to put her finger on it, she hugged him back. It wasn't just the physical attraction, which was amazing, but there was something else. Suddenly it dawned on her. She actually mattered to him. She could feel it. That was the difference. Richie had never cared for her beyond the first physical attraction, if he ever did. How had she not made that distinction before?

"So, did you like the costume?" she asked feeling more sure of herself.

"Yes, I did."

"Better than the dress?" she teased.

"I have to be honest. I still dream about that dress, but the best part of the dream is that it's you in it." He kissed her then, long and slow with the wind pushing against them. He broke the kiss with a groan.

"You'd better go. Your friend will be worried and Rosie is probably tearing up your house."

Shouts coming from the park reminded them that they weren't alone. A few people, including the Mayor and Helen from the post office, were waving their hands and shouting in his direction.

"Shit." Evan sighed then put his forehead to hers. "Straight home." He reluctantly let her go. "Get Rosie. Then to Serena's. Text me when you get there." He opened the door for her to get in.

"Yes, sir. See you soon." Claire said as she slipped behind the wheel.

"Keep that costume handy." He winked at her.

She smiled up at him and answered, "You, too, Deputy."

Evan laughed then started walking towards the park. He couldn't hear what they were shouting over the wind but he could tell by their grim expressions something awful had happened.

CHAPTER 21

The first drops of rain started to fall as Claire pulled into her driveway. She hurried from her car to the front door, but stopped short when she reached for the knob. Relief flooded through her when she felt it was locked and had to use her key. Slamming the door behind her she called out, "Rosie, I'm home."

She looked around and noted there didn't seem to be anything knocked over. Hearing a movement in the bedroom, she hurried down the hall to comfort the scared dog.

"Rosie. We're going for a ride. Come on girl!" Claire called as she leaned forward to look under the bed. The click of the bedroom door shutting behind her made her stomach drop to her feet.

"You're not going anywhere," a familiar voice said from behind her. Claire turned to see Richie leaning against the door with a wicked looking blade in his hand. "Where is it?"

"What?"

"Stop playing games, Claire. Did you find it? Is that how you bought this house?"

"I don't know what you're talking about."

The first slap with the back of his hand stung, but she held her ground.

"I don't know what you're talking about and hitting me isn't going to help."

"We'll see about that." The second blow sent her flying back onto the bed. Claire tasted blood.

"I don't know what you want. Why don't you just leave me alone? You don't love me."

Richie's harsh laugh seemed to echo through the house.

"Love you? You stupid bitch. I never loved you. You think I came all the way to bum fuck swampland for you? Don't be stupid. You took something that belonged to me and I want it back."

"What?" Tears stung her eyes. "Tell me what it is, so you can take it and leave. I don't want you here."

Claire looked around frantically hoping to hear Rosie in the hallway. There was no sound but the rain pelting the house and the low rumble of thunder.

"If you're waiting for the dog. She's gone."

He paced back and forth in front of the bed the blade shimmering in the flashes of lightning. Claire choked back a sob. Rosie. Her sweet Rosie.

"It's your fault. I should have been long gone by now."

The hatefulness in his voice had her sobbing uncontrollably. How could he have hurt Rosie? She wouldn't have hurt a fly. She covered her face with her hands.

"You would have never known I was ever here, but it's not here. You found it. Didn't you?"

"Found what?" she choked out between sobs.

Nothing was making sense to her. She had made

sure she took nothing of his when she left. She wanted no reminders of the painful years they had spent together.

"Where's the table Claire? I've been through the whole house. Twice! It's not here. What did you do with it?" He was screaming now, his face twisted with anger.

"Table?" She sat straight up on the bed. "What table?"

He was crazy. She could see it now even in the dim light. His eyes were wild as he looked at her as if for the first time.

"The side table with the broken drawer that I fixed for you," he said softly as if talking to a child. A shiver passed down her spine.

"That's not yours," she said flatly. Then her anger began to grow. "You came all this way and killed my dog for a table?"

Screeching she flew at him. She managed to make contact with his cheek, scraping his skin with her nails before he shoved her back down again.

"You are a stupid bitch! It's not the table, it's what's in it. In the hidden compartment. Did you find it?" Richie growled at her as he hit her again. This time using his fist.

When she could speak she asked, "Hidden compartment?"

"Where's the table?" he demanded again.

In the midst of all the drama, she had forgotten the table wasn't even there. Serena had it. She laughed through her now swollen lip.

"It's not here."

"I know that. Where is it?" Growing impatient he grabbed her up by her hair. "Don't tell me you got rid of it."

"No. I didn't."

Claire was thinking of how to get the table for him without dragging Serena into this mess. Let him have the damn table and whatever was in it. She didn't care. She just wanted him gone.

"Look, let me go get it. I can go get it and bring it back to you, so you can leave. No one has to know you were here."

"Do you think I'm stupid? I let you leave and you'll go running straight to your cop boyfriend. No, you'll take me to it and you're gonna do it right now."

"Only if you promise to take the table and leave and not hurt anyone else."

"No, Claire. This is how it's going to work, since you don't seem to understand. You'll do as I say, and maybe no one else gets hurt. How's that?" He yanked her hair for emphasis. "Where is it?"

"My friend borrowed it for the festival. She still has it."

"Then let's go get it."

He pushed her towards the door. Once she opened it, he grabbed her arm and drug her down the hall.

"Where's your keys?"

"In my purse." She motioned to where she had dropped it by the front door.

"Get 'em. Just the keys. Leave your phone here."

She bent over to pick up her purse, hoping to grab her phone without him seeing. Her costume didn't have pockets, but maybe she could stick it in the waistband of the skirt. Before she could wrap her hand around it, Richie snatched the purse from her hands. He fished out the keys and threw the purse back on the floor spilling the contents. Claire watched helplessly as her phone skidded across the floor and under the flowered sofa.

"Let's go." Richie motioned with the knife towards the door.

Between her tears and the rain assaulting the windshield, Claire's vision blurred. She didn't even care. Rosie was gone. She had thought Richie could no longer hurt her. She had been so wrong. She would do whatever he wanted just to get rid of him. Serena should be at home waiting for her, so she planned to just go in and ask for the table. Serena was expecting her to stay and Rosie was supposed to be with her. A sob escaped as she thought of her dog.

"Would you knock that crap off?"

"Why did you kill Rosie? She wouldn't have hurt you or anybody. I don't understand."

"I didn't kill your damn dog." He snorted. "Just like you though to pick the most useless breed on earth."

"She's not dead?" Claire asked hopefully.

"No, she wasn't the last time I saw her. Just worry about getting the table back, Claire."

"Ok." She sniffed. "She lives out of town, but she has it. It's not going to be a problem. I can just go in and get it for you. That way she'll never even see you. Nobody has to know just like you wanted," she reasoned.

"Kinda late for that. Your boyfriend knows about me. He had my car staked out and he's probably looking for me now. Maybe he's found the surprise I left for him back at the festival."

"What are you talking about? What did you do?

You better not have hurt Evan."

"Don't worry about that. Just drive."

"Then you'll leave, right?"

Suddenly Claire knew it would never be that easy. She thought of all the things she could have done. She could have tried to call someone if she could have sneaked her cell out of her purse. *Of course, there was no where to hide it in this outfit*, she thought as she looked down at the flouncy white blouse now speckled with drops of blood. She had been so upset about Rosie she wasn't thinking clearly. She still wasn't.

She should have driven straight to Evan, but she had no idea where he was right now. The rain had shut down the festival early, so he could be anywhere. She looked over at Richie still holding the knife. She didn't want anyone else getting hurt. A small part of her hoped she could trust Richie to do as he said and just leave. Probably the same small stupid part that kept her hoping he'd change.

It was too late for all of these things. She was at Serena's long driveway. Maybe she could just drive and drive until they ran out of gas. He'd figure it out soon enough, but maybe it would keep her friends safe. She glanced at the knife again and sighed.

As she turned into the driveway, she hoped whatever it was he was after was enough to make him leave, and leave them unharmed. The headlights shone on the front of the old home giving it an eerie glow.

"Your friend lives here?" Richie asked skeptically.

"Yes. Her name is Serena."

"She lives here alone?"

"Yes."

"You'd better not be lying. I don't want any

surprises."

"I'm not. I promise it's just her. She borrowed the table for our booth. If you want, I'll go get it and you can wait in the car." She tried one last time to keep him away from her friend.

"Nice try. So she can call your boyfriend, I don't think so." Richie narrowed his eyes at her and grabbed the keys out of her hand, "Get out."

Claire opened the car door and stepped out into the lashing rain. The storm was in full force now. The big oaks thrashed about with every gust in a mad dance. Claire didn't look back. She ran straight for the front porch. Richie roughly grabbed her arm and yanked her back before she reached for the door.

"Not so fast. What do you think you're doing?" he screamed at her.

"Just trying to not get wet," she snapped back pushing her hair out of her face and gesturing to her costume, now soaked and clinging to her uncomfortably. He pushed her in front of the door and stepped to the side as the door opened.

"There you are! I was just on the phone with Faith. She called to make sure you got here ok. They were worried about you in this weather. I have to say I was worried too, until I saw your headlights coming up the drive," Serena said with obvious relief as she opened the door wider for her friend.

Claire took a step into the light shining through the open doorway. Serena gasped as she noticed Claire's swollen lip and the blood on Claire's soaked shirt.

"Oh my god, are you ok?"

Before Claire could answer Richie stepped out behind her and pushed Claire roughly through the door sending her crashing into Serena. Claire's sandals now covered in mud slid beneath her. She tried to grab onto Serena for support but they both ending up falling to the floor. The heavy door slammed shut and Richie stood over them.

"Give me your phone."

Serena glared up at him coldly as she tried to help Claire sit up.

"Let me guess, you're Richie?"

CHAPTER 22

Evan watched until the flashing lights from the ambulance were nothing but colored blurs through his windshield. A group of kids had found the badly beaten Dale Hicks in the park. At first, they thought he was trying to scare them with fake blood, they had told their mom. Thankfully their mom had decided to go check it out before the rain started or Dale might not have been found until morning.

His keys and wallet were gone, but the viciousness of the attack didn't point to a simple mugging. It had to be personal.

He had to admit when he had seen Dale pawing at Claire earlier, he had wanted to punch him. As much as the guy got on his nerves, he'd never imagine smashing his face in. True, Dale Hicks did not have many fans, but he couldn't think of anyone that would take it this far.

Unless, Richie had been watching Claire, too. His car had never moved. Dale's keys were gone. Evan assumed Richie had taken his car, but it was found parked at the school. It didn't appear to have been moved. The rain was definitely hindering his search for Richie, if he was still out here, he either had a great hiding place or he was getting soaked.

Evan checked his phone again, no new messages. Claire had plenty of time to make it to Serena's, but he hadn't heard from her. After another pass around the park and down main street he figured he'd run by her house just to check on things. He asked neighbors to let him know if either car moved then headed to Claire's.

Evan was relieved when he pulled into the empty driveway. The relief turned into concern when a frantic Rosie ran up to greet him. There was no way Claire left Rosie outside in this weather. He approached the house as quietly as he could with a whimpering Rosie tagging along. Then thought better of it and put Rosie in the backseat of the SUV. Hopefully the sounds of the storm would muffle his entry. The front door was slightly ajar. He drew his weapon as he pushed the door slowly. His concern grew when he saw Claire's purse and its contents scattered across the floor. Then he remembered the mess Rosie had made during the last big storm. Maybe the scared dog had ran off and Claire was out looking for her. Cautiously, he moved to the kitchen. Everything there seemed to be in order. Listening for noises, he continued down the hallway to the bedroom. A rumpled bed and scattered clothes, nothing too devastating. He let out the breath he hadn't realized he had been holding.

He holstered his weapon and took out his cell to call Claire. She'd be worried about Rosie. Punching in her number as he started back down the hallway, he stopped when something crunched under his feet in front of the closed bathroom door. He jumped when he heard Claire's Fleetwood Mac ringtone coming from under the sofa in the living room. Heart pounding, he reached for the bathroom knob and turned it slowly.

His growing concern skipped worry and turned into a full blown panic at the sight that greeted him when he opened the bathroom door. Glass from the shattered mirror and broken bottles littered the floor, but what worried him more was the blood smeared shower curtain that had been ripped from the rod. Fighting the panic, he called his sister, hoping she had heard from Claire.

"Where are you?"

"At home. Where else would I be in this weather?"

"Is Claire there?"

"No. She's at Serena's."

"Are you sure?"

"Serena said she was driving up when we were on the phone. What's wrong?"

"Rosie was out again. Claire's house is open. Her purse and phone are here, but she and her car are gone."

"Oh, well that doesn't make any sense but Serena said it was her pulling up. Maybe she just got in a hurry and left everything. You know, to beat the rain."

"Including Rosie?"

"No. She'd never leave Rosie out in this weather. I'll call Serena back."

"Give me the number. Stay home. Don't come over here.... and don't go to Serena's."

"What? Why?"

"Dale Hicks was attacked and is in the hospital."

"Oh my god. But what does that have to do with Claire?"

" ...and someone was bleeding all over Claire's bathroom."

"Evan, do you think it's Richie?"

"Yes. I do. I've got the sheriff's office on the lookout for him as a person of interest. I'll have them be on the lookout for Claire's car, too. So stay put. I'm going out to Serena's. I'll call for back up when I'm sure they're there."

"Call me when you know something. I don't like the idea of you going over there alone."

"Well, I can't call for back up until I know where they are. Stay put."

Evan secured the front door and headed out to his SUV in the raging storm. He tried calling Serena's number from the road several times, only to get her voicemail each time. Cursing he pushed the end button again, looking up in time to see a fallen tree branch through the heavy rain. Evan swerved violently to miss it, his SUV almost spinning out of control. Rosie yelped as she hit the back of his seat.

"Sorry, girl," he said as he put down his phone and gripped the steering wheel tighter, "We've got to get there in one piece or we won't be much help."

A whimper from the backseat was his answer.

CHAPTER 23

 "Where is it?" Richie growled grabbing Serena's phone from her hand. "Where's the table?"

"My table, just give it to him." Claire put a hand to her bruised face wincing in pain.

Serena nodding, answered. "Ok, it's still in my car. I didn't have a chance to unpack before the rain started."

"Where's your keys?"

Serena pointed to the table in the foyer as she stepped in front of Claire. "It's not going anywhere. Why don't we wait for the rain to stop? It's really storming out there." Serena tried to talk him into waiting, but he couldn't be reasoned with.

"Let's go." The blade flashed as he waved it in front of him. "Don't try anything stupid."

Back out into the driving rain they all went. Claire and Serena were drenched as they struggled to get the table out of Serena's car and into the house. The weight of the table combined with their slippery hands made it hard to hold on to the edges. Several times the heavy table slipped through their fingers, dropping to the ground. Claire could feel one of the curvy legs weakening with each smack.

Leaving a trail of dripping water as they hauled the table into the parlor, Claire kept an eye on Richie. He paced around them muttering, flinging water from the cape as he moved. After placing the table down, the girls stepped back nervously waiting to see what Richie would do next.

Serena nodded to Claire, then shifted her eyes toward the mantel. Heavy brass candle holders in various heights adorned each side of the hand carved mantel. Claire nodded back understanding what her friend meant to do.

The table wobbled under his weight as Richie yanked the drawer out and dropped it on the floor. Claire had no idea there was a secret compartment. She knew the drawer stuck sometimes, but had never thought much about it. She had asked Richie to look at it once and he had fixed it or so he said. It was one of the only good memories she had of him. She should have known his eagerness to help had nothing to do with her. He had found a secret compartment, and had obviously hidden something in it. Mesmerized, Claire waited to see what was so important.

He felt around in the opening with his hand until they heard a click. His hand reappeared clutching a stack of money. His eyes glittered wildly as he held up the cash muttering to himself.

Claire was fascinated by the pile of cash. She sensed Serena trying to get her attention but couldn't take her eyes off of the money. *Her table.* She had carried that money through two moves without even knowing it was there.

Richie stole a quick glance at the girls, his eyes bright with greed and suspicion. As if unsatisfied with the size of his stash, he jammed his arm elbow deep into the table scratching around violently.

Suddenly back in the moment, Claire turned to see Serena edging a hand along the mantle, her eyes locked on Richie's back. Frozen in helpless terror, she watched as her friend's fingers wrapped around the base of a heavy brass candlestick.

Claire sucked in a sharp breath, immediately regretting it. Richie paused at the sound, but before he could turn, Serena swung the candlestick in a short vicious arc to the back of his head.

Money flew as Richie collapsed onto the table, snapping the weakened leg. Richie hit the floor hard, flipping the table on top of him.

Not waiting to see if he would get up, Serena grabbed Claire's hand and ran through a cloud of swirling cash to the kitchen. Claire scrambled to keep up, still slipping and sliding in her muddy sandals.

"Get those shoes off, quick," Serena hissed.

She motioned for Claire to follow her up the service stairs. When they reached the second floor, they could hear the screaming and cursing. Serena guided her through the top floor around paint buckets and tools.

"When he comes up the service stairs, we can go down the main stairs. If we can get to my room, we'll shut the fake wall and wait him out," the fear in Serena's dark eyes mirrored the fear Claire felt.

Richie's obscenities and threats of what he was going to do to them had Claire shivering. After all that she had been through this night, she knew without a doubt he wasn't bluffing. A part of her still hoped he'd take the money and just leave. *What is wrong with me?* she thought as she hugged herself to stop the shaking.

They heard when he found the stairs. If his ranting hadn't given him away, the clattering from the stairs would have. His wet shoes squished and slipped on the newly varnished stairs.

They left their hiding spot and silently descended the main staircase, passing back through the parlor to Serena's room. Once inside, Serena shut the bookcase wall leaving them in darkness.

"Where's the light switch?" Claire whispered desperately feeling along the wall.

"No, don't. He may see it under the door. Hang on a minute." Claire could hear Serena moving around searching for something. "Damn, I wish he wouldn't have taken my phone. Where's yours?"

"He made me leave it at home."

"I think we need to wait him out."

A scratch followed by a hiss, then a soft glow appeared as Serena lit a candle. They could hear him above pacing on the landing. A door slammed. They heard Richie let out a curse then two sets of footsteps. Serena smirked, "I think my ghosts are going to keep him busy."

Claire thought frantically, they couldn't stay here forever. She knew without a doubt Evan would come looking for her but his shift wasn't over until dawn. Faith thought they were here safe, so no one would be sounding the alarm just yet.

"Look, if I lead him out of the house into the woods, you can make a run to your car and go get help."

"No, we need to stay together," Serena shook her head, her wet curls limply framing her face.

"Listen, he has my keys. We can't use my car. If I get him out of the house, you can go find help."

"No, we'll both go. I'm not leaving you here." Serena hissed her dark eyes flashing.

Claire considered then asked, "Do you have your keys? Maybe we can make a run for it."

Serena hung her head. "He took them when we went to get the table."

"Is that the only set?" Claire asked hopefully.

"No, I have a spare set somewhere in the kitchen."

"I'm not chancing you getting hurt. It sounds like he's on the landing. I'll run out and make enough noise so he'll hear me. Don't come out until he leaves the house."

"I don't like this." Serena said grabbing Claire's arm.

"He'll find us eventually, and there's only one way out of this room." Claire gestured to the door.

Serena shook her head solemnly, "Ok, but run down the path. There's an old tool shed not too far. Maybe you can throw him off and double back. Come back in here and hide until I get back." She hesitated then added, "Maybe I should go instead."

"No, he'll come after me. I know it. Besides, I wouldn't even know where to begin to look for the keys." Another door slammed upstairs.

"I know you're up here, you stupid bitch! I'm gonna find you and when I do I'm gonna gut you like a pig!" Richie threatened.

Serena pulled the latch to open the book case and Claire slipped out. Creeping softly through the parlor, she looked down at the scattered money and her broken table as she passed. It made her sick and angry. She stopped at the foot of the staircase listening. A door opened and closed somewhere above. A sudden rush of fear made her want to run back to the safety of the hidden room. Looking back at Serena through the crack in the bookshelf door, she took a deep breath and stood up straight.

"Richie!" Claire bellowed, "I've got your fucking money and you can't have it back."

Then she ran for the front door and slammed it behind her. She ran without looking back, her bare feet smacking the wet ground, splattering her ankles with mud. The rain had slowed but the wind pushed at her. She ran blindly into the darkness, slowing when she could no longer see. She hadn't thought about bringing a light or anything. Her feet were hurting from stepping on rocks and sticks. She tried not to think of what else might be underfoot as she cursed herself for not grabbing a pair of Serena's tennis shoes.

She stopped and listened for Richie. It was so dark, he wouldn't see her unless he had a light. She waited, hearing nothing but the sound of the wind and rain pelting the leaves on the trees around her.

A loud crash to her left sent her stumbling blindly away from the noise, hands out in front feeling for anything in her way. She didn't dare stop even though she was terrified. Serena hadn't said how far the shed was. It felt like she'd been shuffling forward for hours but in the darkness she knew her senses couldn't be trusted. The blackness closed in around her. Branches and brambles scratched at her ankles and arms as she pushed them aside. Trying desperately to stay on the small cleared path, she felt for it with her bare feet. She felt like there was a crushing weight on her chest. She fought to breathe, hoping to calm the panic that was rising in her. She startled at a sudden flash of lightning. Just ahead, she thought she could make out a structure. She ran for it hoping to take cover.

Richie was in an upstairs bedroom chasing down another slamming door, when he heard Claire holler at him. He wasn't hearing things. They must have split up. That closet door had slammed shut. He knew he had heard it, but when he opened the door there was nothing inside. It had to be some kind of trick or something. After the front door slammed, he looked out the window to see Claire running out into the darkness.

"No, you're not getting away this time and not with my money," he snarled running for the staircase, knife in hand. Cursing and muttering, he stumbled over paint buckets and trays in his path.

As he approached the landing, he heard another door slam behind him. He turned in mid stride at the noise, his foot barely settled on the first step of the sweeping staircase. There in midair, as if caught in a tiny whirlwind, a single hundred dollar bill fluttered eerily in front of him. A violent force slammed into his back, sending him head first down the stairs. Throwing his arms out too late, he twisted his body to make his back take the worst of the impact. A fatal mistake he realized. He felt the knife plunge into his chest as his feet flew over his head and he tumbled end over end down the stairs. Even through the blinding pain his anger raged on. His last thought before he lost consciousness was of Claire trussed up like a hog hanging from a hook.

Serena listened from her secret room to the ruckus above. She had left a crack in the bookcase so she could see when he descended the stairs and left the house. Suddenly the noises stopped and it became eerily quiet. Was he in the parlor waiting for her? She thought she saw a shadow pass but wasn't certain. She listened for the front door opening, but there was only silence.

They hadn't thought Claire's plan out all the way. What if he didn't leave the house? She couldn't chance being caught with Claire out in the woods. What if Claire came back too soon and he was waiting for her? They would definitely be worse off. She wished she would have thought to grab the candlestick again or something she could use as a weapon. She hunched forward watching and waiting to catch a glimpse of Richie or at least a noise to alert her of his whereabouts. Her pounding heart and her own breathing were the only sounds she could hear.

CHAPTER 24

Evan sped up the long driveway. As he approached the old house, his headlights caught a flash from Claire's tail light reflectors. Relieved but still cautious he cut his own lights, slowing his cruiser to a crawl. He let out a breath and parked behind her car. Rosie was still whimpering in the back seat, but he wasn't taking any chances of letting her loose again. The weather alerts had been coming in frequently. The whole area was under a flash flood warning. The thunderstorm system was as wide as it was long and covered most of the state. Now it was the least of his worries. He thought of Claire again and the blood in the bathroom. He was not willing to lose her on the same day he had finally admitted to himself that she meant something to him. Heaven help Richie if that was her blood.

Exiting his vehicle quietly, he crept up to the front door listening for voices. Hearing none, he moved over to the sidelight to look inside. There was no mistaking the outline of a crumpled body at the bottom of the stairs. Instinctively, his hand went to his sidearm. From the weird angle, he couldn't see a face or even hair. It seemed to be covered by a black cloth of some kind. His gut hurt as he prayed it wasn't Claire. He wanted to rush in and make sure it wasn't her but he didn't want Richie to know he was there just yet. He thought about going around the back of the house, hoping to get in unnoticed, when suddenly the front door opened. He flattened himself against the wall and braced to take down whoever appeared. No one did. Ever so slowly, he crept around to the doorway peering to each side. He saw no one. As he took a step inside to get a better look at the crumpled figure at the bottom of the stairs, he heard his name.

Automatically, he spun toward the sound, his weapon coming into firing position. He swept the area, taking in the overturned table, the floor littered with cash and the bookcase swinging open.

"Shit!" Evan let out a breath as he holstered his weapon.

"Where's Richie?" Serena whispered emerging from the bookshelf. "I heard the door. Did he leave or was that you?"

"It wasn't me" he breathed, turning to examine the body, "and I don't think Richie is going anywhere."

Serena approached, leaning over Evan's shoulder gasping as she saw Richie laying awkwardly at the bottom of the staircase. Evan lifted up the black cape that covered him to reveal the knife protruding from his chest. He checked for a pulse, finding none he turned to Serena for an explanation.

"He must have fell. I was waiting for him to go after Claire but he never did. I thought he was just waiting us out."

Evan had been looking back at the money, but at the mention of Claire's name he looked around trying to process what he was seeing. "What exactly have y'all been up to here? Where's Claire?"

"What do you mean?" She narrowed her dark eyes at him and pointed at Richie's body. "*That* monster came here for the table. He had hidden money in it. He brought Claire here to get it. You didn't see her. Oh my god." She put her hands to her chest, "The dream. There was blood on the white dress..." She looked at him with her eyes wide and pleading.

He hung his head. "There was blood at her house. That's why I came looking for her."

"Then it was dark and I couldn't find her..." she whispered as tears streamed down her face. "Claire's out there now in the woods." She turned towards the door.

Evan grabbed her arm. "No, you need to stay here. I have to call this in and then I'm going to find her. I need you to stay put and explain what happened. Don't touch anything, ok?"

After calling the station to request an ambulance and the coroner, he went back to where Serena leaned against the wall. Gazing through the sidelight into the darkness as if willing Claire to appear, she mumbled to herself.

"Ok, I've got people coming. They're not far away. Explain it to me. Why is Claire in the woods?"

"She ran down the path to the shed to make Richie follow her. To get him away from the house. I was supposed to get my keys and go for help when he did. But I never saw him. I thought he had finally went out when I heard the door, but it was you."

A weight lifted off of his shoulders. If Claire was able to run, she couldn't have been hurt that bad. She was alive and he would find her. He was still reassuring himself when Serena's last statement registered.

"Are you telling me you didn't open the door?"

"No. I didn't. I was in my room behind the bookshelf listening for him to leave."

The hairs on the back of his neck stood up. He looked around again.

"Somebody opened this door. Is there somebody else here?"

Before she could answer somewhere upstairs a door slammed followed by the faint sound of footsteps. He reached for his gun.

"No, it's no one," she said softly putting her hand on his arm.

He looked at her incredulously. "Are you telling me you didn't hear that?"

"I hear it often." She turned back to the window, her reflection a mask of sadness. "We've got to find her. I thought maybe she'd come back now. If she sees you're here, there's no reason for her to stay hidden."

He was still trying to process what he had just experienced when the flashing blue and reds came racing down the drive. Evan went out to meet the arriving officers and explain what he had found.

He wasn't surprised to see the Sheriff's truck in the lead. A dead body meant press. Kermit Bourque was here to make sure it wasn't bad press.

"Bertrand!" Kermit blasted as soon as his door opened. "What the hell is going on here?"

"Got a body inside." Evan said as he approached the Sheriff's truck.

"Did you shoot him?" Kermit's voice was so

unusually low, Evan wasn't sure he had heard him right.

"What? No. He was dead when I got here."

"Squirts said you been looking for this guy since this afternoon. He's been bothering your girlfriend or something. If you did this, I can't help you, son." Kermit shook his head worriedly.

"I didn't do this and I don't have time to argue with you Sheriff." He turned on his heel to walk away, "I have to find Claire."

"Bertrand!" Kermit bellowed at his back. Evan didn't bother to turn around.

Grabbing a flashlight from his vehicle, he heard a whimper from the back seat. He had forgotten all about Rosie. He let her out and walked the frightened dog up to the porch where Serena waited.

"Where did you find her?" Serena asked as she bent to hug the dog.

"At Claire's running loose."

"Bertrand, is that what I think it is?" Kermit barked as he strode onto the porch without using the steps.

"Yes, Sheriff. It's the dog that wrecked into the post office. I don't want to chance her getting loose again."

"Do I need to remind you this is a crime scene, not a kennel?"

"Nothing's been touched inside. It's exactly like I found it." Evan cast an angry glare at the Sheriff then turned to Serena. "Keep her out here until they clear the house."

"Sure. Come on, hun." Serena guided Rosie over to a patio chair as Evan started down the steps.

"Where do you think you're going?" The Sheriff's

thunderous voice echoed under the porch. "I'm gonna find Claire. She's out in the woods."

"Wait. I've got a call out to Fire and Rescue. They're getting volunteers to come help."

"You can wait, and get your picture taken. I can't just sit here." Evan strode off into the darkness leaving the red faced Sheriff to take over.

Evan started down the trail, flashing the beam of light in front of him and calling out to Claire. Serena had explained that she was supposed to stay on the path to the shed, so at least he had a starting point. The wind and rain would probably muffle his voice but as long as there was a chance she'd hear him, he'd keep calling for her. He tried to calm himself. Panicking wouldn't help either of them now. He had to find her. He felt terrible that he hadn't kept his promise to Claire. He hadn't been there to keep Richie from hurting her, but he could try to make it up to her by being there from now on. The beam of light hit on the old tool shed ahead of him. He vaguely remembered this being here from his teenage years. There was another path that lead to the river. Recalling the flash flood warning, he hoped Claire didn't go down to the river. Or the river didn't rise up to find her.

"Claire! Claire!" He called out as he pushed on the old door. "Claire! It's me. Are you in there?"

The hinges had rusted after years of nonuse. After a few rams with his shoulder, he got it open only to find nothing inside but cobwebs and rusty tools. There was no way Claire would have been able to open that door. He went back outside to walk around the back of the shed. Calling out again. He listened for any sounds of movement, but only heard the thunder and howling winds.

Retracing his steps, he kept hollering her name and flashing the light through trees as he did, hoping to catch her attention. He kept walking, hoping somehow that they had just missed each other. He made it back to the house only to find she still hadn't come back.

Outside, the volunteers had started to gather on the porch, rain gear ready. Inside, the coroner was loading the body up to be taken to the morgue as other deputies gathered up the evidence.

He found Serena in the kitchen. After giving her statement, she had changed into dry clothes and made coffee to keep herself busy.

"No luck?" she asked worriedly.

"No." Evan reached down to pet Rosie. "Would she have went anywhere else? Maybe to a neighbor's?"

Evan watched as the huge dog padded over to a pair of muddy sandals left in front of a door. The dog sniffed at the shoes and whined loudly.

"I don't have any close neighbors, you know that."

Rosie let out a series of woofs.

"She's been doing that since she got here. Come on baby, she'll come back soon." Serena tried to comfort the dog. "She wouldn't have ran down the road in this weather." She shook her head again as she thought. "No, the plan was for her to run down the path to the shed, so I'd have time to get to the car and leave."

Evan let out a frustrated sigh. "Could she have taken the wrong path and went down to the river?"

Serena paled. "I guess it's possible. I've never taken

her down that way. So she didn't know about it, but if she got confused in the dark..." she stopped and turned to stare out the window as Rosie pawed at the shoes, "...in the dark."

Evan went out to join the fire and rescue volunteers that were waiting for instructions. Not waiting for the Sheriff, whose booming voice was still barking orders inside, Evan directed the men to concentrate their efforts toward the river trail. The sternly urgent faces that returned his look were ready to get to work. This was one of those times he loved being from a small town. Neighbors were always willing to help in a crisis. He knew all of the men here and he knew they wouldn't give up until they found Claire. Even his old friend, Jake was among the group.

He recognized his dad's truck pulling into the driveway and sighed. Faith had probably worried them all to death and his mom had probably made his dad drive out here to check on things. He waited for his dad to get out of the truck so he could explain and was surprised when Faith came running through the rain.

"What the hell, Faith? I told you to stay put. You have no business driving in this mess."

"What did you expect me to do? Wait at home making myself sick with worry? You never called and no one is answering their phones." She pointed a finger at him angrily.

"Kinda busy here, Sis," he growled through clenched teeth. Her anger faded as quickly as it erupted.

"Are they ok?" she asked worriedly.

"Serena's in the kitchen with Rosie. She's shook up

but she'll be fine."

"And Claire?"

He couldn't look at her when he answered so he looked at his boots. "We're trying to find her."

"What do you mean? Her car's here."

"She's in the woods somewhere. We're going out to search now."

"Ok. I brought Dad's boots and slicker in case I needed it." She turned back towards to truck.

Evan heard a chuckle from behind him. "Damn it Faith," He lowered his voice as he grabbed her by the arm, "I didn't mean you."

She turned to face him. "I want to help."

"I don't need someone else to worry about right now." His dark eyes pleaded with her.

"I'm sorry Evan." She sucked in a breath as she looked past Evan then quickly looked away. "I'll go find Serena. I'm sure she's going nuts." She patted his hand then hurried inside the house passing the Sheriff on his way out.

"Where are they going?" Kermit asked noticing the men leaving the porch and headed to the woods.

"We're going to search down towards the river."

"I'm in charge here, Bertrand. Not you."

Evan's swift advance caught the giant man off guard. His face inches from the Sheriff's huge eyes, as he backed him into the door.

"I don't give a damn about who's in charge. All I care about is finding Claire and nobody is going to stop me, Sheriff," Evan said through clenched teeth, his eyes glittering dangerously as he waited for a response.

Kermit, red faced and uncomfortable, gave a nod. "Go on, then."

CHAPTER 25

Equipped with rubber boots and flashlights, they set out in the rain. The closer the search party came to the swollen river without finding Claire the more scared he became. He remembered an old dock where they used to hang out at and drink. It was probably rotten by now and not safe to walk on. He started to imagine all the terrible things that could have happened to her. Out here, with the water rising, the snakes would be moving to higher ground. He couldn't imagine why she'd still be hiding. Surely she would have noticed all the lights and know it wasn't Richie after her. Unless, something happened that she couldn't see the lights. He cursed to himself. He couldn't think like that. He would find her and she would be ok. They came to the edge of the swiftly moving river. Shining their lights across the water searching for any sign of Claire. Serena had said she was still in the costume. He desperately looked for the white of her shirt in the muddy water.

He wanted to scream and rage just like the storm around him. He wasn't giving up on them, not yet. He regretted staying away from her the last two weeks. He let out a curse as he turned looking in a different direction. Some of the men had started to backtrack just to make sure they hadn't missed her somehow.

He felt someone's hand on his shoulder and turned to see his lifelong friend Jake regarding him with concern. "Hey, man, you ok?" he shouted to be heard.

"Yeah, I just don't understand where she could be."

"I told them to keep searching here. Let's take a couple of guys and go back from over where we started to the shed?" He motioned back towards to the house.

"Yeah, good idea. We can cover more ground. Thanks, man."

"Don't worry. She's out here and we're going to find her."

He nodded and turned back towards the house flashing the light before him in a wide pattern.

The rain seemed to slow and then began to finally die down. The front had finally pushed through and the temperature would start to drop now. He hoped now Claire would be able to hear them hollering her name. He motioned to the other men to start moving in the direction of the shed.

As he neared the edge of the woods, he heard shouting. Running towards the noise he found Faith. Dwarfed in her father's slicker and rubber boots she reminded him of how she looked as a child playing dress up.

"What are you doing out here? What's wrong?"

"It's Rosie. She keeps pawing at Claire's shoes and whining. Now she's scratching at the door."

He remembered the muddy sandals and how the dog was acting in the kitchen. "Those were Claire's shoes?"

"Yes, she took them off when they were hiding from Richie. Do you think Rosie could find Claire?" she asked hopefully.

He shook his head uncertainly. The dog was an overgrown walking mess. Could she be trusted to find Claire or would she get lost in the darkness too?

"I don't know," he answered both questions.

Then he remembered Claire telling him that Rosie liked to play hide and seek with her. He didn't know if they ever played outside in the dark but he thought it was worth a try.

"Let's see what she does. I'll follow her so she doesn't get lost."

They walked back to the house. Rosie was scratching at the door, her loud woofs muffled through the wood. Serena came to the door.

"Should I let her out?" she asked through the sidelight. Evan nodded in agreement and readied to follow the dog hoping she wouldn't lead him on some wild goose chase.

"Ok, Rosie go find Momma!" Serena commanded as she opened the door.

Rosie sprinted forward not stopping to jump on Evan or Faith but running straight past them. He followed behind her pointing the beam of the flashlight as far in front of the dog as it would reach. Rosie ran down the path towards the shed. Evan caught up with her as she stopped suddenly, back tracked a few feet and tramped off to the right away from the river. Evan felt a little relieved and assured by this new direction. If Claire wasn't in the river, they had a better chance of finding her. He could hear someone behind him, but didn't dare take his eyes off of Rosie. He knew without a doubt it was Faith. She wouldn't have stayed at the house waiting this time. Flashing the light ahead he could almost see a path, it was overgrown but still shorter than the brush surrounding the trees. Rosie went on ahead, not in a straight line but weaving back and forth from one side to another. Evan pushed at branches that blocked his way. Somewhere along the way he noticed more light from behind him, but he never looked back.

Rosie suddenly sprinted out ahead disappearing into the darkness. Evan cursed and ran after her not caring about the branches that slapped at his face. When he didn't catch up to her, he forced himself to stop and call out, "Rosie!"

Two loud woofs answered, leading him to a small clearing. Illuminated by the beam of light, he found a small graveyard littered with several weathered headstones and what looked to be a large above ground tomb. An unmoving Claire lay at the foot of the tomb, Rosie nudging her. When Claire didn't move, the great dog simply sat next to her on the muddy ground, shivering. Evan ran the rest of the distance to them shouting Claire's name.

Tears of relief stung his eyes as he dropped to his knees next to her. He put the flashlight on the ground pointing in her direction and gently turned her face towards him saying her name again. His stomach rolled as he looked down on her swollen bruised face. He was reminded of the first time he saw her in the rain with her soaked clothes and those big blue eyes. He wished she'd open them now. He needed to look into those eyes and know that she was ok.

"Claire, can you hear me?" he asked desperately. He felt for a pulse, holding his breath. He thought he felt it, but couldn't be sure.

"Claire," he said again as he lifted her shoulders from the mud trying to rouse her. It was then he noticed the wicked gash on her forehead. A few tears broke free and slid down his cheeks. He lifted her limp body to him and awkwardly tried to stand back up. His feet slipping upon the muddy ground, he turned toward the light that had appeared behind him.

He heard his sister cry out as the beam of light found them, "Oh, Claire. No! No! No!"

"It's ok Faith. I've got her. She's going to be ok." Evan tried to reassure his sister. Then said it again willing it to be so. "She's going to be ok. Somebody shine the light for me. We've got to get her back to the house."

More lights appeared down the trail. Evan moved as fast as he could toward the lights without dropping Claire, not slowing until he saw the house with the ambulance waiting in front.

Evan placed her as gently as he could on the waiting gurney. The EMT's loaded her into the ambulance and began to check her over. As Evan watched on helplessly, he felt a push on his leg. Rosie sat against him and whimpered. Serena came rushing from the house to stand beside him.

"Is she ok?"

"I hope so. She's got a nasty cut on her head. Looks like she fell in the graveyard and hit her head on a headstone." Now that his hands were free he wiped at his eyes. Tears or rain, he wondered to himself.

"Graveyard? What graveyard?"

"Yeah, I was just as surprised as you."

An EMT approached. "We've got her stable, but we really need to get her to the ER."

"I'll follow you to the hospital." Evan spun away heading to his SUV.

"Sir, she's coming around. Asking for Evan?"

"That's me," he said pushing his way past to enter the ambulance.

"Claire. Claire. Can you hear me, darlin'?"

"Evan," Claire said his name in a hoarse whisper.

"Yeah, I'm here."

"Richie...here..." Claire tried unsuccessfully to lift her arm. "Serena."

"It's ok. He's gone. Serena's ok. She's right here," Evan said taking hold of her hand. Serena hearing her name popped up into the cramped space.

"I'm here, hun."

"Serena. Gardenias. I smelled them. It's going to be ok."

"Yes, everything's going to be fine," Serena reassured her friend. "They have to take you to the hospital right now. I'll be there as soon as I can."

"Evan," Claire whispered through her swollen lip. "Sorry about the costume. It's ruined..."

Evan laughed and wiped the tears of relief that had escaped. "Don't you worry about that. I'll buy you a new one. Whatever you want. I promise."

CHAPTER 26

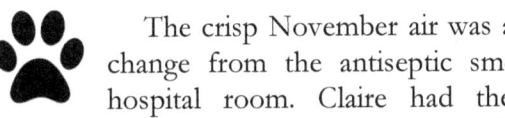 The crisp November air was a welcome change from the antiseptic smell of her hospital room. Claire had the window down and was enjoying the fresh air as Evan drove her home. Somewhere along the way he had taken her hand. She smiled down at their joined hands and thought about the last few days. He had barely left her side.

The events of Halloween night were like a bad dream. She had been so relieved to know that Serena had not been harmed. Her sweet Rosie was alive. Richie on the other hand was not. Claire regretted how it had ended with Richie, but knowing that he would never bother her again was a weight off of her shoulders. She would never have to hide from her past or be afraid it would show up on her door step.

Claire had given her statement to the police. After finding their keys, Serena's phone and Dale's wallet in Richie's pockets, the police had ruled Richie's death an accident and all of their items were returned. The money was a mystery to Claire as well as to the police. Claire told them about the table and Richie finding the hidden compartment. She recounted his ravings about the money but he had never said where he had gotten it or who it belonged to. The money was taken into evidence until the police could conclude if it had been stolen. Claire didn't care. Her friends were safe. She was happy to have escaped with only minor wounds that would heal. Her lip was still sore. The cut on her head had needed stitching and would take a little longer to heal. Her bruised ankle would only have her hobbling for a few weeks. Evan had already volunteered to play nurse when he wasn't working. She grinned, then groaned as her cracked lip protested in pain.

"What's wrong?"

"Nothing. I'm happy to be going home."

"Well, do we need to go right home?" he asked mysteriously.

"No. I guess not."

"Are you sure? If you're hurting I'll take you straight home."

"Where do you need to go?"

"It's supposed to be a surprise. You've got some people waiting to welcome you back." Pain or no pain, she grinned ear from to ear.

"Really?"

"Yeah, but don't go crying just yet. It's supposed to be a surprise."

"Ok, what did you tell them?"

"I said I would tell you we were picking up Rosie from Serena's, but if you're not up for this, it can wait," he said gently, then added with a smile, "My pushy little sister can wait."

"I'm fine and we do have to get Rosie. I know she misses me." She leaned her head back on the seat.

"Ok, but if you get tired or start hurting tell me."

"Promise."

Driving up to Serena's house, she wasn't sure how she would react after everything that had happened there.

She was worried for nothing. As soon as the house was in sight she couldn't help but smile. The late afternoon sun chased away any bad thoughts. She was excited to see their colorful tent set up in front of the house and her friends were waiting on the porch with Rosie. A handmade banner strung across from the tent to a column sweetly welcomed her home.

Her friends-- her new found family. Claire realized now that she had grabbed on to them like a branch or a lifeline. She was holding onto them for dear life and wasn't letting go. This was her home now and these people were her family. She wasn't lost anymore.

Rosie adorned with a flowered collar ran to greet them as Evan came around to help her out of the truck. She couldn't stop the tears as she hugged her sweet dog. Serena and Faith waited for her to hobble to the porch. The smells of fresh baked pumpkin spice cake with cream cheese icing and coffee filled the crisp air. The table was set with china and a fancy white tablecloth.

"Welcome home!" Trent and Hannah exclaimed jumping from the tent.

"Y'all are so sweet," Claire said through teary eyes.

"Come and sit." Serena held a chair out for Claire.

"What's with the tent?" She laughed as she sat heavily.

"We wanted this to be a happy day for you and to make it a good memory."

"Oh, it is. It is." As she took it all in, she caught a glimpse of her table within the tent. "Is that my table?"

"Yeah, Dad fixed it. He's been working on it nonstop to have it ready for when you got home." Faith grinned at her.

"Where are your mom and dad?" she asked as she looked towards the house.

"They thought it might be too much to have everyone here at once. She'll check on you after you're home, but if you need anything just call."

"They should have come for cake." Claire pouted.

"Oh, and mom wanted me to tell you that she has gumbo waiting. Evan can go pick it up when you get hungry." That made Claire smile.

"I'll pour the coffee. Faith, you cut the cake," Serena directed then asked, "How are you feeling? Are you ok?"

"My head hurts, of course and the pain meds make me groggy."

"I knew I should have brought you home." Evan gave his sister a dark look.

"No, this is wonderful." Reaching for Evan's hand Claire pulled him to sit in the chair next to her. "I'm glad you did this. Serena are you ok?"

"Of course. I wasn't hurt, just scared for you."

"No, I mean…" She pointed to the house. "what happened….he died here. I didn't see the body but you were here and…."

"No, none of that today. We'll only have good thoughts. You are home safe. He is gone. This place is my home and it will be a place of peace." Serena finished pouring the coffee then looked at them all. "I wanted all of you here for this." Serena went into the house and came back carrying the sign they had found in the closet. "I had this cleaned and restored."

She turned it so they could all see. The black script lettering could be easily read and the life like gardenia flowers seemed to bloom around the letters. The wooden scroll work that framed the edges had been antiqued with black and gold paint.

"I still have a lot of work to do here but I've settled on the name. Coeur du Bayou. I'm trying to research the history of the house, but I think that this was the name. I love this house. My heart is here." She looked around the table at her friends and smiled. "I want everyone who comes here to feel at home. So, I think the name fits."

"This is beautiful and it does fit," Claire said softly.

"What about the ghosts?" Faith asked wide eyed.

Evan shook his head in agreement. "Yeah, they'll be running the guest out of here with all that door slamming."

"You heard it too?" Claire asked curiously. No one had filled her in on everything that happened that night.

"Yeah, pretty freaky." He smiled at Claire then turned to Serena. "I wouldn't be advertising that feature."

"Oh, but people would come. They have waiting lists of people that want to stay at a haunted bed and breakfast." Faith sat across the table with her piece of cake.

"Yeah, till doors start opening and shutting. Then they're running for the hills." Evan took a bite of cake and smiled. "This is good, Sis. I have to tell you I was definitely spooked when that door opened right in front of me."

"No, I have a feeling this will work out just fine. It's all falling into place." Serena looked around her then sipped her coffee.

"When will you open?" Claire asked between bites of cake.

"Maybe in spring... I don't know. It's taken me a while to figure out what exactly I want it to be." Serena shrugged.

"It's beautiful and when I'm feeling better, I can help with the painting or whatever you need."

"Don't worry about that. You guys enjoy your coffee and cake. Faith and I will be right back."

Trent and Hannah ran off around the house, with Faith and Serena following them. Evan looked at her and smiled.

"Are you sure you're ok with this?"

He wasn't sure that bringing her here so soon had been a good idea. She hadn't seen Richie at the bottom of the stairs. Neither had Faith. The coroner had taken the body before Faith had showed up. He was glad for that.

Serena had seen it. Remembering the look on her face, he knew she wouldn't be forgetting it anytime soon. After everything, she was still here. That said something about her. What it said, he wasn't sure.

"Yeah. I'm glad to be out of the hospital, and I'm glad we came here. Your family is so good to me, Evan." Claire wiped at her eyes.

"Tears, again?" he teased.

"I'm sorry." She sniffed and looked away.

"Don't be. It's all right."

"You don't understand. I want you to know that if it doesn't work out between us, that they still mean the world to me."

"What are you talking about? Dumping me already?" He laughed nervously.

"No, I just don't want you to feel pressured because I love your family so much. They've done everything to make me feel at home here. If I'm intruding, you have to tell me," Claire said through the tears.

"Claire, look at me." He sighed as he held her hand and looked into her eyes. "They love you because you are loveable. They loved you before I even knew I loved you."

Claire questioningly searched his face then accepted the answer she found there. Smiling she agreed, "You do."

"Yes, Claire. I do." His dark eyes were gentle and filled with so much warmth and desire she had to look away.

Faith and Serena came back outside both holding candles. "We have something else we need to show you."

"What?"

"We want you to see where you were the other night."

Claire gulped loudly looking at the fading light. "It's going to be dark soon. I don't know," she said nervously.

"We have lights and I've had the path cleared. We've waited for you to do this. We thought you'd want to be here."

"I don't understand."

"It's too much. She can't walk that far." Evan pushed his chair back to stand. "We can do this later."

"We thought of that too. Trent! Hannah!" Faith called to her kids.

The kids came around the side of the house

pushing a wheelchair decorated with flowers that matched Rosie's collar.

"Come on Claire. Let us show you what you found," Faith urged.

"What I found?"

"Come on, Miss Claire. It's so cool."

"Well, we have to be cool." Claire smiled at Trent and with Evan's help made it to the wheelchair.

The fall light was beginning to fade. The darkness would come fast. Faith handed Claire a blanket to cover with since she didn't have a jacket. They started down the path and Claire remembered running for the shed.

"The shed? But you knew that was here. It was so dark. I couldn't see anything. I didn't think to bring a light. It was so dark," She said again remembering.

"This is the path to the shed but you somehow turned off and went this way," Serena said pointing to another path lit with solar lights and candles hanging from garden hooks.

"We lit the candles all the way down so we won't get lost," Hannah said proudly.

"Thank you. I don't want to get lost again. That was scary."

"You don't have to be scared. We're all here." Trent walked closer to her. "It's neat and Miss Serena said we can come visit when we want. I might even have a camp out here sometimes if Uncle Evan comes with me." He glanced hopefully at Evan.

Evan laughed. "I said I'd think about it, squirt."

The path continued on. Claire was amazed at how far she had went in the dark. It all looked so harmless now with the path cleared and lit up. They finally reached a clearing and Claire couldn't believe what lay ahead. A graveyard. A small graveyard. It had been trimmed and cleared out. The graves all had flowers and candles.

"I don't understand," Claire said taking it all in.

"We had no idea this was here, Claire. These graves might give me some clue to the history of the house." Serena explained as she put her candle next to one of the graves.

"We decided to have our own candlelight service since we missed All Souls Day." Faith rearranged some flowers in a glass vase on one of the graves. "I loved that when we were little. We would actually have a candlelit mass in the graveyard in town. Remember that Evan?"

"Yeah, I do, but mostly because we got to run around in the dark." He laughed.

"You didn't know this was here?" Claire asked Evan.

"No, funny no one came across it in all these years, but you found it somehow in the dark." Evan smiled down at her. "You probably tripped on one of the headstones and hit your head on another one when you fell."

Claire put a hand to her head touching the bandage as she tried to remember. "Yes, the bigger one there. I saw it when the lightening flashed and I thought it was the shed. I remember running. I don't remember anything else but the smell of gardenias." She looked around the edges of the graveyard. "There's got to be a gardenia bush around here it was so strong and it reminded me of…" Her voice trailed off as she looked around to Serena. Evan squatted down to look at her.

"What? It reminded you of what?" he asked gently.

"The day we found the sign, we smelled gardenias. Remember?" she said looking at Faith and then Serena.

"Yeah, I'm not likely to forget that day," Faith said looking around. "But I don't see any flowers. I don't think that blooms till the spring anyway."

"I haven't smelled it again. I wonder what that means," Serena said thoughtfully.

"I don't know but I smelled it and I knew everything would be ok."

"You girls are killing me with this shit. First the dream stuff, then tarot cards and then the door slamming ghosts. Halloween's over. Enough with the spooky shit."

"Evan," Faith hissed.

Hannah giggled as she danced around the clearing with Rosie chasing her and Trent smiled at his uncle.

Serena just laughed and hooked her arm through Faith's. "Enough for now. It's a mystery that we obviously won't solve today, but we've got another piece."

"Come on, darlin'. Let's get you home." Evan stood to push Claire back down the path. "I promised to take care of you and I keep my promises."

Claire smiled into the darkness as he wheeled her away. She knew without a doubt that he would.

ABOUT THE AUTHOR

Lisa Coots grew up in the tiny Louisiana village of Lacassine, but has always yearned for the challenge of a new adventure. Her youthful dreams ranged from the artistic: as a sketch artist and painter; to the studious: as a writer and librarian.

Lisa's dreams were nudged aside, as dreams often are, by conventional reality. Marriage and motherhood came easily to her and she successfully raised three remarkable children and an amazing husband. When the first pangs of empty nest syndrome came a rapping, she eagerly returned to the artistic passions of her youth; painting, designing, and of course, writing.

Lisa Coots now lives in a slightly larger village in Louisiana with her loving family and lots of furry friends.

LisaCoots.com